Jonas

ROBINSON DESTRUCTION BOOK 5

KATHI S. BARTON

This is a work of fiction. Names, characters, places, and incidents are products of the author's imagination or are used fictitiously and are not to be construed as real. Any resemblance to actual events, locations, organizations, or persons, living or dead, is entirely coincidental.

World Castle Publishing, LLC
Pensacola, Florida
Copyright © Kathi S. Barton 2021
Paperback ISBN: 9781955086578
eBook ISBN: 9781955086585
First Edition World Castle Publishing, LLC, July 12, 2021
http://www.worldcastlepublishing.com
Licensing Notes
Cover: Karen Fuller
Editor: Maxine Bringenberg

Chapter 1

Jonas sat in the office and waited for the doctor to finish up with Hailey. He was glad that he'd asked Rogen for help in finding him a good psychiatrist for the child. At only ten, Hailey was having more difficulty than the other kids. Her lack of trust was beyond anything he'd ever seen in his life. Even his brothers, who were both doctors, were worried for her.

The door opened, and Hailey came out, with the doctor right behind her.

"He said I'm insane." Jonas looked at the doctor, who was laughing while shaking his head. "Well, he might as well have said it. He thinks I'm not telling him everything."

"Are you?" She shook her head and turned to look at the doctor before looking at Jonas. "That's all right, honey. Whatever you need to do, I'm right here for you."

"You say that, but then you bring me here. Why?" He told her, deciding that lying to the kids was going to hurt them all in the long run. "I have my reasons. Why do I have to share them with a stranger?"

"Will you tell me?" She looked back at the doctor, then at him again. "Hailey, have I given you any reason not to trust me? At all? If I have, then you have to tell me what it is. I can't fix what I don't understand."

"That's what Ms. Tru said. That she can't fix what she doesn't understand that is broken. Do you think I'm broken, Mr. Jonas?" He said he didn't know, that he didn't want her to be afraid of everything. "I'll have to think about it."

When she walked back to the doctor, he got down on her level. Dr. Miser was supposed to be the best child psychiatrist in the world. He hoped so. Jonas really was afraid for his children and their mental well-being.

"I'll come to see you. But I don't trust you." Dr. Miser told her that he was well aware of that. "I know you are. But I'm not going to give you that until I'm sure. I'm not insane—you know that, don't you?"

"I do. More than you do, I think. You have some trauma that you're not dealing with well, but I think with time, the two of us can get to some sort of conclusion. I'm not going to make you trust me, Hailey, but I am happy that you're at least willing to have an open mind about it." She told him point blank not to put his horses before the cart just yet. "I promise you I won't. But I do see a lovely little girl that has had more than her share of things happening to her that never should have. Also, you might find this hard to believe right now, but you couldn't be with a better group of people than the ones you are right now. They wanted only the best for you and your brothers and sister, and they hopefully found that in me."

As she returned to him, Jonas was so happy when she took his hand into hers. She would do that on occasion, but not often enough for his heart.

As they were making their way to the car, he saw that Rogen was there waiting on them. Rogen was large enough with child that he worried about her just walking around. But like the rest of the men in his family, he didn't say a word to her.

She asked Hailey how the appointment went. All four of the children were coming to see the doctor now. Even Sarah, the youngest of the children, seemed to be coming along better with his help. The only holdout was Hailey. Tru had told Jonas that he should search her mind for the issues, but frankly, he was afraid of what he might find there.

"It was all right. If you're here to drop that kid, then I'll help you. I helped my momma deliver Sarah.

I'm not one to faint with blood all over me." Neither of them said anything to her, but Hailey seemed to realize she might have said too much. "Mr. Jonas said he'd take me to lunch if I didn't murder the doctor like I wanted to. Are you going to join us?"

"I'd like that. Are you really going to murder the doctor? I have to tell you, he's a good friend of mine, and while I can understand wanting to murder a doctor, he's been a good man so far." Hailey said that for now, she wasn't going to. For some reason, Jonas wasn't reassured by her comment, but she got into the car and strapped in. "She's going to be a lot to handle when she does spill out what she's holding to her heart. I thought you'd like to know that I've talked to Sissy Whitman and her father. There is a sister, Ginger, that is around, but she's out of contact with most of the world. I'm trying my best to narrow down what it is she does, but she's off the grid most of the time. How are you doing?"

"Great now that they're all not sick. I've hired a nanny—thanks for the suggestion. Sarah is coming along nicely now that she has her diaper rash under control. Thomas and—" She told him she'd asked about him. "They are mine, Rogen. I find that I can't function without them around me. I know they're more than likely going to be adopted by their aunt, but I love them with all my heart right now, and I don't know what I'm going to do without them."

"Benny Whitman is in jail. He hit his wife, Sissy, in the face and did some pretty painful wounds to her head. That was only the second time he'd hit her, but it was enough for her to call in her father. You know Heath Morgan, don't you?" Jonas said he did. "I thought so. Thatcher said you'd done some work for him a few years ago. Sissy is his daughter."

"I wonder how that will affect whether she is interested in bringing the children home with her. They're a great deal to handle. I'm sure she can afford the help she'll need." Jonas had to turn away. Thinking about the kids leaving him was almost too much for him. "I really love them, Rogen."

"I know you do. We all do." He nodded and opened the front passenger door for her to get into his car. "I can't ride with you—I have my car over there. However, I'd love to join you. I have some things on the burner at home that I need to care for. I'll meet you wherever you're headed."

He laughed as he was getting into the car. If she said burner, he knew for sure it wasn't on the stove. Rogen had about a dozen computer monitors going at any given time that she worked with. Jonas was happy that she was willing to meet him. People looked at him oddly when he was out alone with one or all of the kids like he was some sort of pervert.

Hailey was getting better about going out to lunch with him. So long as she didn't drink anything but bottled water, which he brought with them all the time, she was able to eat things that were hot. Pizza, so far, was her favorite meal. Tru had told her that if there were any poisons in the pizza or anything associated with it, it would be cooked out in the oven. It had taken her three times to be able to eat an entire slice. Now, however, she wanted her own personal pizza. He'd never seen a kid like her food to be so spicy that even he couldn't get close to it because the smell burned his nose. Tru and Hailey would have contests about how hot they could handle it.

They were waiting on their food when Rogen turned to Hailey. "I found out what made the four of you sick that day at the apartment. It wasn't anything you could have avoided. What I mean is, it wasn't poison like we thought, but the vitamins that Cindy was giving you each day. For some reason, they were sold expired. They should have been tossed out about a year ago. Not her fault either. The store they were gotten from should have caught that too." Hailey asked what she'd done about it. "What do you mean?"

"Did you kill them? The people that work at the pharmacy?" Rogen said she'd not thought about it, but if it would make Hailey feel better, she could have them shut down for a while. "No. I don't want that.

But someone should have to pay for making us all sick, don't you think? Mr. Jonas was freaking out, and then he had to call in his mom. Who I like, by the way. She doesn't understand me, but she is a nice person."

"My mom loves you very much, Hailey. All of you." She nodded but didn't comment. Jonas asked about the stash. "I was just curious if there was any word on how it was stored where it was."

Thomas and Bobby had moved nearly five-thousand pounds of drugs from the back of a semi-truck trailer to one that had been sitting on the lot their parents had at one time rented. Having it right there under their noses had been the perfect place to keep it from their father, as his plan had been to sell it all and get himself "better children." Garry, the kids' biological father, had stolen it from some very bad people and the kids, worried that it would kill children like them, had moved it, over a period of three weeks, into the trailer sitting abandoned on the land behind their home.

"It's been stored away. We did it on our own, so there is no trace of it on any books. The thing is, no one has said a word on the streets about it being missing. That's what we're hoping for. Some idiot comes along and starts spouting off about how he's been robbed." Jonas asked if that had happened before. "Sure. For the most part, bad guys are stupider than fuck."

"Packer. That's his name." They both looked at

Hailey when she spoke. "What? Did you think we'd be out of touch with what was going on in our home? Never that. If we didn't pay attention, we'd be hurt for sure. I don't know anything more about him, but that's what his street name was. He would come around the house when Mom was away at some jail, and Dad would tell this Packer guy that he didn't know shit about it."

"Do you happen to have any idea what he might look like?" Hailey said he had tats on his face. One of them was an ugly unicorn or some kind of horse. Rogen pulled up her phone and fiddled with it as their food was brought to them. "Is this him?"

The whispered way that Rogen was talking to Hailey worried him a great deal. He didn't want the kids involved in this. However, he also knew that Rogen and the rest of the family needed help in getting this taken care of before someone else came for them. Also, that even now, they were being guarded with the utmost care. No one would get by anyone in his family to get to the kids.

Hailey took the phone from Rogen and looked at the picture. When she asked if there were more of him, Rogen told her to just flip through the photos there and see what she could find. It was perhaps three or four moments before Hailey handed her back the phone and picked up a slice of her food.

"The man you showed me first is Packer. The second and fourth men in those pictures are always with him. I don't have their names. He usually just nods at what he wants, and they get it for him. I think he might be some kind of shifter person. One time I saw him get all furry like Mr. Jonas does when he's all upset about something." Hailey looked at Rogen as she chewed her food. As soon as she was finished with that, she spoke again. "They carried guns when they were at the house. I helped them move those when we found them. I can't tell you where they are until I talk to my brothers. We made a pinky promise not to tell without all of us agreeing."

"Is there anything else the four of you stashed around? I mean, things that Packer or one of the others with him might have mentioned?" Hailey nodded and continued to eat her food. Jonas was honestly too afraid to eat. He didn't know if he'd be able to keep it down the way that—

"Wait. Did you say Packer got all furry like I do? Or were you just using me as an example?" Hailey told him he was a tiger, just like he was. "Christ. Thatcher can summon him to him if he's not already told him he is in the area. In fact, he can call him to him anytime he wants. Will that be something you can do?"

"I can." Rogen kissed Hailey on the head and got up to leave them. "I'm so thankful for you, Hailey, that if there is a reward for this, I'm going to make sure you get it."

"You can give it to little kids that need it more than we do now." Hailey eyed him. "Unless you want to take it for yourself, Mr. Jonas."

"You four earned it. Whatever it is, you should take it for yourselves and use it for college or something. I wouldn't dream of taking your money from you after all the hard work you've done."

Rogen left them there after waving at the waitress and staff. Not too long ago, he and his family had gotten someone out of this place that was being abused. It was a small world, he thought.

"Mr. Jonas, I have a question for you." Jonas told Hailey that she should just ask him. "We've been around you and your family for two weeks now. You've never once hit any of us or lost your temper. And when we need something, even if it's just an extra blanket, you give it to us. Are you really this nice all the time?"

"I'd like to think I'm that nice. However, as you know, I do have bad days." She said he'd never taken it out on them. "That wouldn't serve anyone if I were to do that, now would it? But in answer to your question, what do you think my mom would do to me if I were a mean person and didn't allow you an extra blanket?"

"She'd beat your head in with a wet noodle." His

mom had said that to him on more than one occasion when he'd been younger. "I'm sort of afraid of her. Not that she's hurt me or anything, but she could, I think."

"Mom would die before hurting anyone. Unless they were planning to harm any of her babies. To her, you are all her babies." She shoved away her pizza, and he was happy she'd been able to eat all but one slice. "If you're ready, we can head back to the house. I'm to understand that Bobby is going to have my brother come and visit him today."

"Why do you care?" That gave him pause, and he asked her what she meant. "Why are you so caring, Mr. Jonas? No one else gave a fiddle about us. You're nothing but a stranger, and you've done more for us than anyone ever has before. Why?"

"I have an answer for that, I think. I love you guys. I know you've heard me say that to you before." She nodded. "All right. I tried to get your mom in a place where she could take care of you if she wanted, but I have since changed my mind about that. I don't think she'd be any better to you than your father was. And I want you four as safe as I can make you. Is that a good answer for you? I can go deeper if you want. But I know how much you hate when I get mushy."

They were both laughing as they went out to the car. This time when he looked around, Jonas could see the men following them—their guards. He'd never been one for people hanging out with him or around him, but he felt a good deal better knowing they were there. Driving home, he decided he was going to take his mom up on her offer to get him a staff. Having people helping with the kids was nice, but he had a feeling that if staff were there, he'd have a lot less stress in keeping up with things.

~*~

Sissy was just getting home from the grocery store when there was a knock at her back door. The only person that used it was family, and when she opened the door, thinking it'd be her father, she was so happy to see her sister.

"Dad called and left me a message that you were in trouble. Christ, that prick really changed his tune about being around you, didn't he?" They hugged several times before Sissy saw that her sister was hurt. "It's nothing. I wasn't paying attention to where I was walking and tripped up on a log. Fell against a boulder and broke my arm. How is your face? You look like shit if you don't mind me saying that."

"I know. People have been pointing that out to me for the last several days. But I decided that getting back to my life is more important than caring about people pointing and staring at me. How are you?"

Telling Ginger to sit down, Sissy made them both a cup of tea. Knowing that her sister didn't care for anything but black tea, she made her a cup. Sissy had a cup of Earl Gray, her favorite.

"Great, but for this arm. I would have been home sooner, but I had to finish up the pictures I was assigned to take. Dad told me you were with him, and I knew you'd be all right. Have you pressed charges yet? That little fucker needs to pay for what he's done to you." Sissy loved her sister so much and was thrilled to have her with her. She told it like it was, and that was just what Sissy needed. "If you'd go with me to take the pictures to the company that asked for them, you and I can get going on whatever it is you've been keeping from Dad."

"How did you know?" Ginger just laughed and said she'd not known. "You've done that to me before, and I can't believe I still fall for it. Yes, I am keeping something from Dad. And I want you to help me with it. Benny's sister? Margo is her name. She is out of jail just recently and wants her children back. That's what caused this last thing with Benny. He didn't want to go get them because one of them might be black. What a fucked up reason not to want them close by. Anyway, I want to go and get them and bring them back here."

"You know I'll do anything for you, but what the hell are you going to do raising a couple of kids?" Sissy corrected her. "Okay, four of them. I'm not saying you can't do it, but Sissy, that's a lot of work. What do you know about them? Much at all?"

"Are you asking me if they're black too?" Sissy knew she'd hurt her sister, and when Ginger stood up, so did she. "I'm sorry for saying that. I know what you're asking me. I honestly don't know what I can do or not. I've never been around children much before. I'm simply stressing over everything I have going on. Please forgive me, Ginger. Please?"

"Don't say things like that to me. All right? You know as well as I do that I could care less about things like skin color and their sexual preference." She hugged her again, and they both sat down. "Do you know where the kids are?"

"I do. They're in Ohio with a family there. It's not a long flight, but we can drive from here if you'd like. Pittsburg isn't a long trip but still too much to do in one day. I think you might be familiar with the Robinsons." She knew that her sister knew the Robinsons and asked her what she knew that wasn't in the background check Dad had done on them a long time ago when she'd gone to college with one of them. "I think you went to school with one of them, correct?"

"Yes. Dawson. He's the youngest. A doctor." She could tell that Ginger was thinking about them. "Can I tell you my opinion about the kids being with them without upsetting you?" Sissy said she wanted her to tell her. "They might be better off with them than you trying to raise them on your own. I love you, Sissy, but as you've said, you don't know a great deal about children. Especially ones that have been around Margo. I can make a call to Dawson, but the last I heard about them, they were taking in children that had been abandoned for a while now."

"All right. Will you call him? Then if he tells us that they're better off with them, I'll believe him. But I'd really like to go and see them. They're my nephews and nieces, and I know nothing about them other than they've been born." Ginger pulled out her cell phone. "I can't thank you enough for this. You don't know how much I've been worrying about them."

"I'd like to speak to Dawson Robinson, please. My name is Ginger Morgan. He and I went to school together." Sissy couldn't hear what was being said on the other end, but when Dawson must have come onto the line, Ginger spoke again. "How the hell are you, dumbass? I didn't think I'd get through to you. I figured you'd be out on the golf course or some other equally stupid shit I've heard about doctors." Ginger told him she was putting him on speaker phone.

"I've not thought of you in…well, I'm not going to say how long it's been. Busy with life. But I do reminisce about some of the antics we were up to. No, not on the course. I don't have time for that now that I'm working for myself. Holy Christ, Gin. I miss you.

Where are you now? Still taking pictures of weddings and grads?"

"No. Wildlife. I just got home and was told that my sister's soon-to-be ex-husband has some relatives that might be in your care. I don't know a great deal about them, but the Feds were supposed to have called Benson a few weeks ago to come and get them. I was hoping that my sister and I could come out and see what we can do about this." Sissy heard the background sounds cut off when a door was shut. "Something wrong, Dawson?"

"I'd say that's an understatement. How much do you know about why we have them?" Sissy spoke up then and told them she knew nothing more than what someone had told her husband, brother to Margo. "Hello, Sissy. Your sister spoke highly of you while we were friends in college. About the kids...I'm not sure what I can tell you over the phone. If you'd like to come out here, I can arrange that for you, but you'd not be able to tell anyone where you're headed or why."

"Is it that bad?" Ginger watched Sissy's face as Dawson said it was about as bad as he'd ever seen it. "All right. You make the arrangements, and we'll head that way. Should Dad come with us? I don't want him left behind if we can help it."

"You give me your addresses, and I'll make sure your homes are watched over." Sissy was starting to get very nervous about this now that it seemed the kids might be trouble. "Bring Mr. Morgan with you too. I'd like to see him again. But just be careful, guys. There is a great deal at stake, and a lot of lives involved that could be endangered should there be any kind of leak out there."

"Call me when you find out anything. In the meantime, we'll get going here. Nothing packed, so there is no reason to think we're leaving. No mail stopped. Nothing." Dawson said he'd take care of it. "Good. Thanks. I'll wait to hear from you."

Twenty minutes after her sister hung up the phone, an officer came by the house. He said he was there to inspect the windows and doors as he'd been asked to do. As soon as he was in the house, the man went through the house and opened the back door, letting several men in with not just guns on their person, but also armor and other very scary equipment.

Ginger was handed a cell phone, as well as a bag. When they were told to stand in the hallway, three men went over the house with equipment, telling them they were to search for bugs and other devices. A camera was set up in the dining room, and they were asked to have a seat. First, however, Sissy was asked to call their dad over for lunch.

Dad was happy to join them. She wasn't to tell him that Ginger was at her house, nor about the people in her home. Sissy was beginning to see that the kids were in deeper shit than even she thought anyone could handle. As soon as their dad joined them, they were asked to go to the computer monitor and have a seat. Someone appeared there almost as soon as they were surrounded by the men that came with them.

"Hello. My name is Rogen Robinson. I work for the Federal Government. My family and I are protecting the children and want to make sure that when you arrive, you're as safe as they are." Dad asked what was going on. "I can't tell you anything right now, Mr. Morgan. Only that the children are safe and that we'll make all the arrangements to have you brought to them. As you've been informed, you're just to leave your home the way you entered. Ginger, you're not on the radar just yet, so when you leave, I'd like for you to go out the back the way you entered and into the woods. The car you drove is no longer parked where you left it, but someone is there you can trust with your life."

"Since you're not giving us anything to work with here, you tell me why I should trust you with my family, Ms. Robinson. They're all I have in this world." Someone entered the picture with them, and Dad asked Dawson what was going on. "They're treating us like we've done something wrong here, Dawson. You know us. We'd never harm a fly."

"Mr. Morgan, had you been even the least bit suspicious that the men in the home with you now were there to kill you?" Sissy asked Rogen if that was necessary to tell them. "It is. I won't lie to you about any of this. I will tell you that the kids are heroes and have been working with us since we brought them here. Once you arrive, you'll stay with my husband and I, and we'll explain everything. For now, you'll do as I asked. The phone that Ginger has is secure. If anything goes wrong on your end, even if one of you are even remotely worried about something, call. The men with you are going to be at your beck and call until you arrive. Trust them as you would each other."

"And if we don't?" One of the armed men came into the room then and put the gun to her father's head. "Are you trying to scare me, Ms. Robinson? I'm made of sterner stuff than having an empty gun to my head."

The gun was fired at the wall and blew a hole large enough that she could see her side yard. Sissy started crying when Ginger stood up and punched the man that had fired in the face. Then while he was falling, Ginger kicked him in the crotch. He went down much harder than Sissy had thought, but Ginger had always been strong. Ginger then stood in front of the monitor.

"You fuck with my family like this again, and I don't care who the fuck you're working for. I'll hunt you down for the rest of my life to kill you. Understand?" The woman laughed and said she did. "Good. My dad isn't healthy, and doing shit like that will hurt him. I will not hesitate to pull the gun from your downed man and kill the rest of them here, even if it means my own death."

"I like you, Ginger. No, I won't pull any more tricks on you."

After Rogen told them again how to leave the house, they did so without any more incidents.

They were on the plane in short order and served not just drinks but lunch as well. It freaked Sissy out a little when they not only had her favorite meal for her but a cup of hot Earl Gray as well. Sissy was even more terrified, thinking of what they did know about her and wondered how much more they knew about her and her family.

Chapter 2

The office she was using was old world, and obviously for a man. Ginger waited for her call to be connected and looked around. The backyard was a place where she thought she could take some really nice pictures. Not that she'd offer them to anyone, especially not the lady of the house, but she'd take them anyway. Finally, Mr. Roads answered the phone.

"I have your pictures right here, Miss Ginger, but I can't use any of them. They're marked up with your name all over the front and back of them." She told him that was so he couldn't use them without payment. "Payment first? Well, I don't believe that is what we agreed on. No, I'm sure of it. I would have remembered that part very well. You send them to me without all these markings on them, and I'll see what I can use."

"No." He didn't speak, so she didn't either. Rogen came into the office and asked her if she minded. Shaking her head, Ginger waited on the man to come to some sort of terms with using the pictures he'd wanted.

"No? That's all, just no? I don't believe I like your tone, young lady. You'll do as I wish, as I am the customer, or I shall not use them at all. And in addition to that, I'll blackball you from ever selling your mediocre pictures again." Ginger just laughed and put the phone on speaker so that Rogen and now her husband could hear. "Did you hear me, young lady? I will ruin you if you don't play ball with me."

"I'm not concerned about you playing ball with me or with yourself for all I care, Mr. Roads. There is something else you should be aware of. When you try and use my photos without paying for them, it will eat your computer system alive. I know this because I paid well for it to work that way. Also, printing them will cost you and will only print my markings, as you called them, and nothing more. Good luck with trying to blackball me."

She hung up the phone and looked at the couple in front of her. There were things she wanted to know, but also things she needed to tell them. Some of it wasn't all that terrible, but a couple of things she had going on were really bad.

"You want to share whatever you have going on in your head?" Rogen was straightforward, and she liked that. It was still debatable whether or not she cared for the woman on a personal level. "We've had you investigated, and there isn't much out there, is there? I mean, other than you taking pretty pictures for magazines. What is it you're hiding from us, Ginger?"

"I started out only taking pictures, pretty ones as you called them. But then I started seeing things that very few people get to when they're out and about. Or I should say things they know what the hell they're looking at. I work for the CIA as an operative that gets in and out of places on the guise of being a photographer. Not that I'm not making good money on that, but I make more working for the government. My handler told me that I could be as honest with you two as I am myself, which really isn't saying that much. I'm rarely honest with myself. I tell myself all the time that this is the last shoot I'm going on and end up right back out there the next week. You're agent 0032."

"I am. You're agent 0134. I'm assuming you've been doing this about as long as I have." Ginger didn't answer her but did look at her cell phone when it rang. Ignoring it for now, she looked at the picture over the mantel, the one of the house they were in. But long ago. "I was going to ask you if you would mind taking a picture of this home the way it is now. I'll gladly pay you."

"No need for that. You're putting us up. For now. What is going on with my sister's nieces and nephews? I was told they're coming to see us today, but I'd like the lowdown on them now." Rogen stood up and asked her to follow her. "You have to take me someplace more secure than this room? I'm assuming you've taken care that none of us are carrying any kind of trackers."

"I didn't have to. After I figured out who you were, I thought you'd done it." Ginger said she had. "All right. Also, you've come back clean on the background check, what little there is out there for the public to know. What does your family know about what you do?"

"My dad knows, but I didn't want my sister's husband to find out shit, so I didn't tell her. I bet that just burned your toast, didn't it? Not able to find out shit on someone." Rogen said it had, actually. Thatcher laughed and then said he didn't know if he could take any more sarcastic women. "I don't plan on staying here long enough for you to get used to any of us."

There was a man down the stairs that looked so much like Thatcher that they had to be related. He introduced himself as Jonas and said he was keeping an eye on the children. When asked why they weren't with him, he said he wanted to meet her and her family before he brought them over.

"There are a couple of things you need to know before you and your family see them. I'm sure you were given paperwork on them, but I want to tell you some things that might not be there. Sarah is not just afraid of the dark, but she will scream until the lights are back on or pass out from fear. A night light doesn't cut it—she needs the overhead on when she sleeps." She made notes on her phone, just in the event this information wasn't brought up tonight. "While Hailey is getting better about food, she's still very particular about what she eats. I've thought about seeing what it is, but I've been taking all the kids to see a doctor to help them deal with the trauma they've been dealt. Bobby is the most outspoken of them, but he still is very good at keeping things to his chest."

"You don't want us to take them, do you?" He shook his head. "I can understand that. They're cute little buggers. However, that will be up to my sister. I don't have any plans of having children, nor do I wish to raise these kids. Not that I won't love them—I will—but with my lifestyle, it would be difficult for me to even be too friendly with them. The bad guys would make what has happened to them thus far look like a day at the park."

"Rogen and Tru told me what you were into—" Ginger asked him if he meant Tru Justice. "She's

Robinson now, but that's her. You know her, I take it?"

"Indirectly. She and Sissy went to school together. I think she came over to the house a couple of times while I was there." Jonas asked her if she was opposed to him being with the kids when her sister met them. "As I said, this is Sissy's idea to take them on. Personally, I think she won't be able to handle it. Not that she'd not try her best, but she's not had any more contact with kids than I have. Not to mention she has a bully of a husband — soon to be ex — that will use them against her in any way he can. While Benny is a lazy fuck, he's not opposed to using people to get what he wants."

"He's in jail now."

Ginger asked Thatcher how long he thought he'd be there. There was something about Jonas that made her pissy and horny at the same time. She needed to get laid, she told herself. But then Thatcher answered her question.

"Not long enough if you ask me. Your sister has some stitches in her head from when she fell back when he hit her. Also, she might not know this yet, but she's going to have a child. I doubt very much she knows that."

"You can smell that on her." Thatcher and Jonas both nodded. "I love Sissy very much, but I just don't see her making this work. I know as I said, that she'd try, but she's much too...how do I say this? Flighty, I guess you'd call it. She tries, but once she gets bored at whatever project she might be working on, she'll move on to something else. And without support all the time, like from myself and my dad, she's going to fail the kids and herself."

"I'd like to adopt them myself." She said she had no problem with that so long as he kept them together. "I'd never dream of separating them. They need each other as much as I need my own family."

"Is she your mate, Jonas?" They both looked at Thatcher. "Ginger, I mean. Is Ginger your mate? I need to know now before the debate about Sissy taking the kids goes on too much longer."

"No." Jonas looked at her, then back at his brother. "If you've all you need from me for now, I'd like to get back to the house. Thomas has a doctor's appointment at four, and he gets anxious when I'm not ten minutes early for it."

Ginger let out the breath she'd been holding since Thatcher asked his question of his brother. When Jonas was gone, she felt stupid for being in a flitter about a man. He was handsome in a rough sort of way. Tall, over six foot, she thought, since she was six-one herself. Jonas also looked like he could eat a bear, make love to a woman, and never muss his hair. Men like him pissed her off.

She looked at the monitor when Rogen said her name.

"The man you were speaking to on the phone this morning, he came across my feed just before you got here. I hadn't read over the report before you arrived but finished it up just before I came upstairs. He's just an asshole that thinks whatever he wants, he should get." She looked at the man and then the things that were in plain sight around his office. "Mr. Roads isn't the sharpest tool in the box, as I'm sure you're aware, and he wanted to have your pictures to compare your style to some others he's come across. Ones that were given to him by another person he has worked with. I don't suppose you'd have any idea what he is looking for. Other than a way to make some freebies off of you?"

"No. I don't. But it's nothing that I've not run into before. But I do have something that I'd like to share with you. A few weeks ago, I was out of the country taking photos of the wildlife there. Monkeys and sloths, for the most part. But there were some things going on that I just happened to fall upon that got the shit shot out of me." She asked if she could use one of her computers. After being given permission, she pulled up her locked file of photos from that area. "At first, I wasn't sure what I was looking for. Or what it was, for that matter. But there was something simply off about the shot."

While they looked for what she'd found, she continued to explain that she was there for photos for a table book that someone else was putting together and didn't have the shots of the monkeys that he wanted, nor a couple of other creatures in the area.

"I don't see anything but trees." Thatcher agreed with his wife that he couldn't see anything. "What is it that you fell on?"

"The electrical conduits that power the place up." After enlarging the photo, she showed them what they'd missed. "The building is cooled by air conditioners that are constantly running. I tripped over the conduit when I got close enough to make out the camouflage covering the building. Army issue and there was a great deal of it. The closer I got to it, the more things I could see."

As she ran through the pictures she'd taken that day, she explained to them both what she'd come across. "There is a mass grave just here at the left of the building. Nothing but body parts fill it. The building itself is a makeshift operating room or something like that. At first, I thought they were harvesting organs. But there doesn't seem to be a rhyme or reason for what they cut out or not. Some of the cutting was going on while the people were still screaming their heads off in pain." Rogen asked where the building was now. "Still where I left it. You're the first person I've told about it. I thought about taking it up with my handler, but there was just too much shit going on that made me wait."

"You think it's one of ours." Ginger nodded as she sat down in one of the many office chairs in the room. "What else did you see that made you think that? I'm assuming that since you were shot up, you must have gotten close enough to see too much."

"They were playing music. Not anything to get your underwear messed up about, but they were singing with it in English. Again, nothing too telling. There was, however, mail on the table addressed in English, and the things that were labeled on the cabinets were also English." Thatcher handed her a bottle of water, and she drained it before continuing. "When they came out of the building to take a piss, one of them noticed that the conduit was no longer covered by leaves. I should have thought to take care of that. But when he pulled out his weapon—with the hand not carrying his small dick—I shot first. On my way out, I was shot a total of sixteen times. Most of them superficial, but they still hurt like a mother fucker."

"Have you had them looked at?" She told Thatcher that she took care of it. "If you'd not mind, I'd like to make sure nothing is festering. I've noticed that you walk with a limp. A small one, but it's there to notice. Also, I'm working as a physician for the government."

"I used to be a registered nurse before becoming what I am now. If I tell you I took care of them, then you can bet I did." Thatcher nodded, but she knew he wasn't satisfied. "There are a couple more things I did before I left the area. I figured out who the people were that the envelopes were addressed to and from. The first piece of mail was from the Pentagon. The second one was from the White House."

"Do you know the names?" Ginger nodded. "Do you trust me enough to give them to me? I'd like to make sure they're not coming from someone I work with."

"Sure. One of them was from you. The second one was from your husband." They looked at each other, then back at her, shock written all over their faces. "The only thing that was wrong and makes me believe you had nothing to do with them was that they had your name as Rogan, with an 'a'. And Thatcher was just plain Thatcher Robinson, no M.D or any other status attached. There was also a small lion, not a tiger, on the envelope, like the person was trying to be funny or some shit. Unless, of course, you were trying to throw someone off. Were you?"

~*~

Jonas waited again in the lobby for Thomas to come out of his session with the doctor. Just yesterday, he'd had Hailey in his office again, and the doctor had told him she was making progress and that he was very proud of her.

Jonas's mind kept going back to the young woman at his brother's home. He'd lied to Thatcher. While he didn't know why he was still trying to figure out how he'd been able to do it. Ginger Morgan was his mate. But for some reason, one that was still a mystery to him, he'd not acknowledged her to Thatcher. Barely to himself.

"Mr. Jonas?" He looked at Thomas and smiled at him when he pulled him from his musings. "You looked like you were sitting there sound asleep. Are you all right?"

"I am. Just thinking hard." Ruffling the boy's hair, he asked him how the meeting had gone. "Did you tell him I forced you to eat broccoli last night, and it turned out that you love it? That was all I wanted from you, you understand. For you to try it. If you hadn't liked it, then you would have known. But you did. So I hope we don't have that fight again."

"I'm sure we will. You make weird food. Nah, I didn't tell him. I did tell him I was sleeping better and that Mr. Thatch and I went fishing yesterday." That had been an adventure, Dad had told him. Fishing with five kids. Dad had been glad they'd been on the dock and not in a boat. He was sure they'd have tipped him into the lake had they been. "Your dad, he sure is funny when he has one of his tales to tell, huh?"

"He is at that. And he's thrilled beyond words that he can tell the same stories he told us when we were little to a whole new generation of kids." Helping Thomas put his hat on, they were headed out the door in a few minutes. "We're having dinner at Thatcher's house tonight. Your aunt will be there."

"She's not really my aunt, is she?" Jonas explained how his mother and Sissy's husband were brother and sister. "I know. Ms. Tru, she told me that while we're not really related, we should be on our best behavior, at least for the first few minutes. Then all bets are off. I think she wanted us to scare her off."

"More than likely. Tru and the others have fallen in love with you guys and don't want you to leave us. But we'll do whatever is right for you guys. I met Sissy's sister today. Her name is Ginger." Thomas asked what she was like. "Beautiful. She's tall too. Not much shorter than I am. Slim. She's got this long beautiful—" Thomas said he was being sappy. "Oh, you don't want to know how beautiful she is? All right. She's a ballbuster. I know you know what that means. She took down an armed man with a single punch to his face, then kicked him in the groin while he was going down."

"Wow, really?" Jonas nodded as he pulled into

traffic. "Kicked him right in the avocados? I can't wait to meet her. Do you think Sissy is the same sort of person?"

"I think she's more laid back, but I think if push came to shove, she'd be able to care for herself. Not a ballbuster, Thatcher told me, but delicate. Like a rose kind of disposition."

Jonas had been using bigger words with the kids, then having them look up what they didn't know. It was fun for them as well as him. When he pulled into the curved driveway, he could see that Hailey and Sarah were sitting on the front step. Bobby was in the rocking chair, and each of them had a glass of something to drink.

He noticed the puppy as soon as he got out of the car. "Where did that come from?" The puppy seemed to hear the sound of Jonas's shock from him being there and curled up behind Sarah. For someone as young as she was, the little girl was as gentle as a lamb with the little thing. "Did one of my brothers drop him off?" He got down on his knees to talk to the little girls. It made them feel safer around him, he thought.

"No, Jamie brought him by. Did you know he's Ms. Rogen's brother? He took our pictures too." Jonas asked why he'd brought him by. "Oh. He's going away for a couple of days and asked if we'd keep an eye on him. Mrs. Hamby is going to make sure she takes him home with her so she can watch him at night. Don't you like dogs, Mr. Jonas?"

"I do, but I'm a cat, you see. Dogs don't usually like being around someone like me." The dog now that he seemed to understand Jonas was no longer upset, jumped at him and knocked him back on his ass because of him being so exuberant to lick him in the face. "My goodness, you're a rambunctious little thing, aren't you?"

As they were playing with the dog, someone pulled into the driveway. He wasn't worried too much. It was one of Thatcher's cars, and when Ginger got out, he felt his heart rate pick up a little too much for what he was doing on the ground.

Ginger came over and sat on the grass beside him and played too. He wasn't sure what she wanted, but he was happy she didn't force her acquaintance on the kids. They, however, seemed to take to her as quickly as they had him when he first met them.

"You lied to your family about me." He said he had but didn't know why. "It took me a little bit to figure out that you had lied. Then I got all bent out of shape, wondering why. As I drove over here, I talked myself out of beating the shit out of you. I don't usually start with something so violent, but today has been an off day for me. Are you going to introduce me to the kids?"

After introductions were made, Sarah made her way to them by holding onto her sister's hand. When she fell, not only did she not cry, but she put out her hands for Ginger to pick her up. Without any hesitation, Ginger stood, then picked the child up to sit down with her in the grass again.

"She's usually not all that good around strangers." Ginger said that technically she wasn't a stranger — she was his mate. "I suppose that could be some of it. You said you weren't good around kids. You handled this well. Better than I did when I first saw them."

"I'm going to convince my sister that the kids will be better off with the two of us rather than her. Also, I'm going to see if I can talk my dad into moving here. You have the room for a few weeks, don't you?" Jonas said he'd make it if he didn't. "Thanks. I'm not one to push away from something when it's a done deal. I'm assuming that with us being mates, it's done and over in that department."

"It is now. I've met you and acknowledged what you are to me. It would be difficult on me to have you leave me if that's what you mean." Ginger spoke to Hailey when she sat on her lap with Sarah. Bobby came over too, but it took him longer to make his way. "They're not shy around you."

"I doubt they would be. Don't you think? I mean, I'm willing to get down to their level and talk to them much like you do." He nodded and watched her pluck a blade of grass from the yard and blow it as a whistle, to the delight of all the kids. "There are a few things I need to clear up with you. I know a lot of shifters in my line of work. Actually, more shifters than humans. Are you the bossy bastard kind that orders women around? Or are you the type that doesn't expect anything more from me than I'm willing to give you? I'm not sure how much that would be at the moment—I don't know you that well. But I'm guessing it will come to that eventually. Me sharing all that I am with you."

"You're taking this a great deal better than I thought you would. That's not true. I hadn't any idea how you'd take this. But I am impressed with you." She smiled at him, and Jonas reacted in kind. "I'm a numbers sort of man that keeps us all in money. I know you have a bit of your own. Not that I've pried, but I know the Morgans. Also that Sissy told Benny she wasn't a part of the 'Morgans' that has money."

"Dad had him sign a prenup. It was told to him that in the event Sissy won the lottery or something, she'd not have to share with him. Or something along those lines." Sarah pulled handfuls of grass from the earth and tried to shove them into Ginger's mouth. "That's all right, honey. How about I take you into the house and get you a clean diaper? You smell really rank."

They were both laughing when she went into the house with Sarah in her arms. Jonas looked at Bobby when he laughed, then asked him what he thought was so funny. Thomas was giggling too.

"You got it bad for her, huh, Mr. Jonas? She's as pretty as you said, but not sappy like you are. Are you going to kiss her?" Jonas told him he certainly hoped so. "Good. I like her. She didn't make us change the diaper, and that makes her all right in my book."

"What would you have done if she asked you to do it?" Thomas shrugged and looked at the front door where his sister and Ginger had gone. "She knows less about kids than I do. I hope we can help each other out until a decision is made about the four of you."

"Me too. I don't want to live with Sissy and my uncle. I don't like him at all." Jonas said they were getting a divorce. "I might be little, Mr. Jonas, but I know that don't mean doddle about people hurting you. Some people don't care a fig about what a kid wants or doesn't want either."

"Did he hurt you guys, Thomas?" He didn't think the little boy was going to answer him. But finally, he turned to look at him and nodded. "I see. Have you told anyone else? Do they know what he did to you guys?"

"He hurt Sarah really bad. Hailey too, but she got away from him. I thought about telling that guy we have to go see, but I don't think I trust him not to take us from you. Not yet anyway." Jonas knew the baby had been raped, but not by who. It was one of the reasons she was terrified of the darkness. Scary, she called them, hurt her. Hailey was not just afraid of food, but looking into her mind, he found she was terrified of being left alone. "Mr. Jonas, if you marry Miss Ginger, will you two keep us safer? I like it here. And I know the others do too."

"I don't know what's going to happen with us, Thomas. I wish I could tell you that you will stay here with us, but I need to talk to a few more people. Also, when we go over to Thatcher's house tonight, Rogen wants to talk to you guys." He nodded. Thomas seemed to like Rogen, but he didn't trust Thatcher. He did like his father, however. "My dad and mom will be there too. You know how much you like them."

"I do too." Bobby turned and looked at him. "Can you carry me in the house, Mr. Jonas? I'm powerful tired, and I'm hurting a little too. I don't want one of them big pills that make me go to sleep forever, but just a little shaving off of it."

The three older kids worried a great deal about medications and how they didn't care to take them. If Bobby was asking for something for pain, then he really must have needed it. Standing up, he picked up Bobby and made a game of carrying him into the house. Hailey went up the stairs where Sarah's room was, to no doubt check to make sure her sister wasn't being harmed. A few minutes later, Ginger and Hailey were talking as they entered the living room where they were. The television was on, but it was on a nature channel rather than cartoons. The only one that enjoyed those was Sarah, and she bored easily with them. When Ginger sat down on the couch next to him, Sarah was put on the floor to go with her brothers.

"Did you know the baby has been hurt?" The whisper was just loud enough for him to hear Ginger, and he nodded when she put out her hand. The small nip, just on the fatty part of her palm, made it so the two of them could speak without the kids hearing. *I've seen injuries like hers before. Men like that need to know what it's like to be butt fucked with something larger than their arm.*

Jonas burst out laughing. He had no idea what he thought was so funny. It wasn't, not at all, but the way she just put it out there like it was something she was really going to do had caught him off guard. He told her who it had been, and she asked if he was where she could get to him.

No. He's in jail. Not that I don't agree with you on what needs to be done to him, but I'm thinking since none of the other women know what happened to her or who did it, you might have to beat them to the draw on taking the man to task. She snorted, and he laughed again. *Thank you for the laughter. I've been so stressed out for the last several weeks that I think I forgot about fun in the world.*

He's mine just so you know. When I find him —Christ, he's the father of my sister's child, and he allowed this to happen to them? Oh well, I'll have to figure out some clandestine way to take him out. I'm sure I can. Jonas told her he didn't doubt she could. *Thanks. I'm going to have to have a long talk with Sissy. She's not going to be happy about the shit I have to tell her, but she's going to know before too much longer. Happy or not, she's going to have some hard-assed decisions to make regarding Benny. What a stupid name for a grown assed man.*

Jonas laughed a great deal that night. Before going to his brothers', he was feeling better than he had in a while. Taking Ginger's hand, he kissed the back of it, much to the amusement of the kids, and got them all seated. Jonas was happy beyond words when Bobby allowed Ginger to get him buckled in without any fuss. This might well be the road that he needed to be on, he thought. One that wasn't nearly as bumpy.

Chapter 3

Sissy wasn't sure how to interact with the kids. They were sort of standoffish and quiet. It occurred to her that they were with Ginger more than anyone else in the household, but she didn't put much stock in that. Ginger was just a likable person. Dad seemed to be at a loss as well.

"Hi, kiddos. How's it hanging?" Sissy stared open-mouthed at Rogen when she spoke to the kids in such a manner. But they laughed and told her they were hungry. "There are some snacks in the kitchen for you all, but first, I want to talk to you about the drugs and guns you found."

"I'm sorry. What did you just say?" Rogen explained how the kids, in trying to keep drugs off the street, had moved a great deal of drugs, nearly a semi full of them, from the place their father had hidden them. "You mentioned guns too. Where on earth would they have gotten this information?"

"Their father." Rogen looked hard at Sissy as if she was telling her to drop it for now. So when she got down on her knees in front of the kids, she handed them each an envelope. "This is the money the government gives to people that do what you guys have done. I split it four ways because I thought that even though the girls didn't lift it, they still helped by keeping an eye out for anyone coming by."

Thomas handed his envelope to Ginger. "Don't you want to see how much it is for yourself?" He told her whatever it was, he'd like it to be put into a college fund for himself. The other kids, except Sarah, did the same thing. "That's an excellent idea. But I think you should each take just a small part of it and get yourself something special. What you four did was an amazing thing, and you deserve some kind of reward for it."

"Mr. Jonas gives us what we need. And when we ask for something, he gets it for us, as long as it's not dangerous and won't hurt one of us." Thomas pointed to the checks. "I don't care how much it is. We did it so our dad wouldn't be able to sell it to people that would die. He didn't care who died so long as he had money to get him a new bunch of kids."

"He didn't mean that. I'm sure you misheard him, Thomas." Thomas turned to Sissy and stared at her for the longest time before he finally turned away. "Rogen, you don't believe he said that to them, do you?"

"I do. Because when he was arrested, again, he said the same thing to one of my officers. That he was going to find the shit, his words, that the kids had taken from him and buy himself some new ones. There is also something else you should be aware of, all of you. Their father hurt these kids in ways that will turn your stomach." Dad asked if he'd abused them sexually. "Yes."

The one word hung there for several seconds before Rogen turned to the kids again. She handed them all a second envelope and told them what it was for. Guns. Not a few either, she explained to Dad when he asked, but several hundred of them that had been carried by the children from a place they'd been hidden to another place, to keep them from being sold.

"You did this? All of you?" Dad watched them as each one, including little Sarah, nodded. He thought she was mimicking the other children, but it did solidify what he needed to know."I don't know what to say. I do know I'm very proud of the four of you. It must have taken you a long time to do something like that. Not to mention bravery. Whatever that amount is on those checks isn't nearly enough as far as I'm concerned."

Rogen laughed. Sissy just didn't understand these people at all. Just as she was thinking she couldn't wait to get home with the children, Ginger spoke up. When she stood up, so did Jonas.

"I'm going to be staying here with Jonas. And if possible, we'd like to keep the kids here with us. Jonas is my mate." Dad stood up and yelled loudly as he danced around with Ginger. Then he shook Jonas's hand until Sissy was sure he was going to tear it off. "Also, Sissy, I have some news for you. You're going to have a baby. The family — they're tigers, as you know — can smell it on you."

"I can't have children." Ginger just cocked her head at her and smiled. "No. I've been to the doctor, and he told me there wasn't much of a chance I'd ever conceive."

"Well, he didn't say you never could, just that you didn't have much of a chance. Congratulations." Dad hugged her as well, but gently. Sissy was still confused as to how she was going to have a child when she realized how the child would have been conceived.

The sting to her face had her looking at Ginger. She'd hit her. Looking around the room, she realized it was just the two of them there. Asking her why she'd hit her, Ginger smiled.

"You zoned out on us. I thought for sure it was because you were going to have a baby, but then you started talking about rape and being tied up. Jonas took the kids out of the room, and the rest of them followed. Did he rape you, baby?" Nodding, Sissy started crying as she held onto Ginger. "I have you now. You've nothing to worry about."

When her tears started to slow, she thought about the things she'd been told and heard the last few minutes. Sissy felt betrayed by her sister. She'd not even wanted to come here, and now she was taking the children from her. Why? Her head wanted to scream at her sister.

"Say it, Sissy. Say it before you zone out again." She did. Sissy told her how unfair it was of her to take the kids from her. "You didn't have them, so I didn't take them from you. But they're happier here than they've been in a long time, and I think that uprooting them now would be—"

"So you decided you'd take them from me and stay here too, with a man you don't know. How selfish can you be?" Ginger stood up and went to the couch across from the one she was sitting on. "As I said, you didn't even want to come here anyway, and now that you have, you think to just take the kids like I didn't want them for myself."

"Why did you want them for yourself, Sissy? A large family is what you've been saying, but I think it's deeper than that. What is it? And I'm not being selfish.

I'm thinking of their lives thus far, and how much it would—"

"I could have moved here for them. I could have helped them out by moving here and raising them. But you didn't even give me a chance at that, did you? You just had to step in and take over. That's what you always do, isn't it? When you think I'm too delicate or something, you just ramrod yourself into whatever it is and take over. I'm a grown assed woman, Ginger, and you're not being fair." Ginger didn't speak, and that pissed her off more. "What is it you think you can do for them that I can't? I'm sure you have a long list of things you think I'd fail at. Tell me what it is?"

"What the hell is up your ass?" Sissy demanded that she tell her what was going on. "All right, no, I don't think you have the support it takes to raise them. Did you know that Sarah was raped by her uncle when he was around? And that her father knew about it? That Hailey has nightmares that have her waking up screaming that someone else is going to come into her bedroom at night and fuck her? That Bobby has cigarette burns over ninety percent of his body? That some of the scars will be there for the rest of his life? That there will be scars on his mind, too, that may never go away? Did you know that someone used his mouth as a sex toy? That they put firecrackers in his mouth and lit them? That Thomas has been raped so many times he's terrified to have anyone but a few people he trusts touch him? That—"

"That's enough, Ginger." They both looked at Dad when he came into the room. "You've made your point, and even though it scares me to no end that these kids have endured this, there is no reason whatsoever to tell Sissy."

"Why? Why are you forever trying to protect me?" Dad asked Sissy what she was saying. "The two of you ganging up on me, keeping me in the dark about shit. Why do you do that? Do you think I'm going to fall apart? That I'm going to fall into some kind of despair now that I've had a glimpse into what those kids have had to do to survive? I'll have you both know that I'm stronger than you think I am."

"Of course you are." Dad sat down beside her. "Sissy, you can't think you can take on four children all alone that have this many problems to deal with. I'm not going to be around forever, and with Ginger getting married, you'll be all alone in this. Not to mention a baby on the way. You've got a great deal on your plate right now as it is. A baby. A divorce coming up. I don't want, any more than Ginger does, for you to be too stressed. Having a baby is hard on a woman. Raising those children will be a great deal to tackle."

Sissy looked at her sister. There wasn't a smirk on her face as she had expected. Not that she'd done that before, but this was different. This was what she had wanted all her life. A big family to hang around the Christmas tree with. Dinners with their families. Now her sister was taking that away from her.

Getting up, she headed to the front door. She knew she was going to regret speaking if she stayed any longer and left the house. She was nearly to the car when Ginger caught up with her. When she asked her where she was going, Sissy turned to her and snarled.

"Don't speak to me." Ginger backed away from her temper that Sissy didn't seem to have any control over. "Just don't. You got what you wanted, and hurray for you. You always do, don't you? Well, I'm going to fight you on this. You'll see that I win, too. Stay away from me, or so help me. I'll find those drug dealers and have them come after you."

"You'll kill the kids too if you do that. Just as quickly as you had put a gun to their heads yourself." Sissy felt her heart crumble. Ginger hadn't cared that she was threatening her, but the kids were first. "Sissy, this is no way to end this. You have to see that."

"What I see is you barging in on things that were never your concern. Don't contact me, Ginger. I'm going to go back home and pretend like you don't exist. I'm sick of coming in second place to you." Ginger told her it wasn't like that at all. "So you say. Goodbye, Ginger. Enjoy them while you have them because I will win this."

She didn't have any idea how she was going to return home. Her purse and all her things were in the house, the one she had no plans to return to. Walking to town had her thinking, and she no more liked the thoughts she was having now than what her sister had done to her. And she had done her wrong, no matter how it looked to her.

Her cell was ringing just as she found a small inn. Pulling out her phone, she saw that the caller was unknown and didn't answer. As soon as she was in the doorway, greeted by a plump woman with a huge smile on her face, she handed her the phone that was on her desk. Answering it, she was embarrassed as well as upset that her sister had gone this far.

"It's Rogen, not Ginger. I must say, Sissy, you've done a bang-up job of upsetting my household. What is it you're planning next? I do hope you know that if you follow through on your plans to turn those kids over to the drug dealers, I'll make your death so long and tortuous that they'll never be able to identify your body with dental records. What the fuck is wrong with you?" Sissy told Rogen she'd not understand. "Then you go ahead and explain it to me. Oh, by the way, when I call, answer. Mrs. Apple has a room for you, but you'll understand that you're putting her and her entire family in danger by your antics. However, I've had to put extra guards around you so that you stay put and keep your fucking mouth shut."

"You can't talk to me like that." Rogen just laughed. "You want to know what happened? Well, I'll tell you what I told Ginger. I'm going home, and fuck you and anyone else that comes along to try and get something from me. Ginger took those kids from me just as surely as if she had kidnapped them. I wanted them first."

"So, because you wanted them first, you think you're entitled to have them. All right. I'll tell you what. Come and get them. I'll talk to Mrs. Apple about them staying there with you, and you keep them with you until you leave here. Or when this mess is over." Sissy asked if she'd be able to take them when she left. "Yes. I'll talk to Jonas and Ginger. They'll understand that you wanted them first. I'll send them over to you since I don't believe they'll be able to walk all that way. Is that all right with you?"

"Why do I feel like you're trying to trick me into something? As I said to my dad, I'm stronger than anyone has given me credit for." Rogen told her that was all right too. "All right. I'll take them. This will be a good time for us to get to know one another before I have to move back home. Because I will take them with me when I leave here."

"Of course you will. If you'd like, before you

leave, I'll set up the paperwork that says you're their mother from now on too. No point in taking them to a courtroom."

This was working out better than she could have hoped for. But she still felt as if she was being tricked into something.

"I'll have them put into a car right now and brought to you. Jonas will have their schedules too."

The call was disconnected before she could ask what kind of schedules. It was probably nothing more than just what time they had bedtime and their eating schedule. Sissy danced around the hallway before Mrs. Apple showed her to the upper floor of the inn.

"There is only one bathroom on this floor. That's why we don't use it much. But there are four rooms here that you can use." The bathtub was a huge one, one that she thought she could soak in for hours. The rooms were pretty. The beds were all made up to look like an old room. No television in the rooms, which she was happy about. There was no point in letting them get used to watching too much television anyway. "You'll be all right up here then?"

"Yes, of course." Mrs. Apple didn't look convinced. "I'll be fine. Just fine. By the end of the week, it'll be just like we were meant for each other."

"You don't have any kids of your own, do you, missus?" She told her that she was actually expecting her very first one. "Well, good luck to you. Mrs. Rogen said that I was to treat you like any other guest in the place and not to make any exceptions. You all right with that too?"

"I am. I'm really glad she mentioned that to you as well. I'm going to have fun. I've always wanted a big family. This will be just perfect. For all of us." Mrs. Apple went down the stairs, shaking her head. "You'll see. All of you will see. This is going to be epic."

~*~

Jonas wasn't happy about this. About any of it. But Ginger told him this was just what Sissy needed, to figure out that she wasn't made to raise four children with special needs. Not that she couldn't do it with just one child, but four was just too many for most people.

"But you think we can." She nodded and looked around the room where they were. There was his family, his parents, as well as a few others that would gladly help if needed. But they weren't going to be there for Sissy. "I don't understand. Why can't we go and give her some help when she needs it? I have it."

"She won't have anyone like this family here once she goes home. My sister needs to learn things the hard way about what is involved in doing what you, with the help of your entire family, have been doing for these little guys. I'm not stubborn enough to think I could do it without help. But Sissy needs to figure this out on her own. Ask Dad. He'll tell you the same thing."

He had. Heath, their father, had told Jonas that he was proud of him for doing this and that he'd better never hurt either of his daughters or now his grandchildren. "Your father, he knows we're all cats, right? I mean, first of all, I'd never hurt anyone unless they were harming one of you guys. Then there is the fact that I can't hurt you, as you're my mate."

"About that—what did Thatcher say when you told him you'd lied to him? I'm sure he wasn't thrilled." Jonas smiled and told her he wasn't pissy at all. Confused but not pissy. "I'm glad. I'm happy about a lot of things right now."

He knew she wasn't—her heart was hurting for what Sissy had said to her, the things she'd blamed on her. Holding her in his arms felt right, but she pulled away too quickly for him, and he asked her if she was all right.

"I'm not. Not at all. But I'm going to be." She looked away as she picked up the jacket that Sarah had worn over to Thatcher's home. "I'm glad your brothers are taking them to her. I don't know what I'd do if they started crying for you. My heart isn't normally so tender, but right now, it feels like it's been stomped on quite a few times."

Jonas had sat the kids down on the couch and

talked to them about what was going to happen. Not that it was a lesson being taught to Sissy, but that she wanted to take them home with her when she left. There had been a great many tears, even his own, but they said they'd be on their best behavior while with her. Hailey was the most afraid, he'd realized. She'd been terrified that Sissy was going to get them hurt. Thomas made a promise that he'd make sure to call if there was trouble. Jonas had hugged them tightly several times before gathering up their clothing and coats.

Once they were gone, it was as if a cloud had settled over the house. Even his mom was caught crying several times when he ventured into the dining room where they were working. Rogen and Ginger were going over the plans for the building she'd found and working to make sure the kids were guarded.

"Benny was released an hour ago. They're still keeping an eye on Margo. I don't think anyone is actually looking for her, but then I haven't any idea what the guys after the drugs and guns know about her. If they find her, it won't be long until they find Benny too. Then Sissy." Mr. Morgan asked Rogen what might happen to Sissy if they found her. "Not to be indelicate, sir, but they'll kill her. After making sure she hasn't any idea where the things are. However, I predict that she'll crack under the pain and tell them where the kids are if they're not with her when they find her. And they will find her. There was several million dollars' worth of drugs and weapons that the kids hid. There is a great deal at stake with this shipment, and they won't be able to walk away."

"But she's out there alone." Rogen pulled up the inn where Sissy was staying and pointed out the people she had there watching her. "You think they're going to strike soon, don't you?"

"Soon? I'd say within the next few days. There are still two people between Sissy and the drugs. Margo is already being watched. And as of the moment Benny left the jail, he was as well. I'm not so worried about Carson, Margo's ex-husband. He's in prison right now on other charges. But I will take care of him too." Heath, as he'd asked them to call him, shivered as if he had an idea what sort of things Rogen was capable of. "The only thing that could mess this up is Sissy getting stupid. The fact that she's out of my range of being able to keep an eye on her worries me, but I have the best men on her."

The limo pulled up in front of the inn while they were watching. Thomas was the first one out of the back, then Thatcher. The other kids, even Sarah, clung to him like he was their only hope. Handing off the children to Sissy was difficult, Jonas could see, but it was when Sissy was handed the envelope that things looked confusing to the other woman.

Thatcher didn't hang around much after that. He did kiss the kids goodbye, then hugged Sarah tightly before climbing into the limo and being taken away. Sissy stood there holding a sobbing Sarah in her arms while trying her best, from what it looked like, to get the others to follow her into the building. There were cameras in the rooms where the kids were staying too, but she didn't bring those up while they were all standing there.

"What happens now? While I love my daughter very much, she's never been like this before. Stubborn, yes, but not foolhardy. I don't want any of them hurt over this." Rogen said she was doing her best to make sure they weren't. "I can see that, young lady. I can. But I'm her father, and I do worry."

"Good."

Heath looked at him. "I hate that you're drawn into this, Jonas. But I suppose jumping in with both feet is the best way to get to know us all. What are your plans for my other daughter?"

"Plans? I have no plans other than to love her and support her in anything she wants to do. I have a good job working for the family. I work at other areas around town that benefits them. If you want to know if I'm going to rule her? Then I can honestly tell you I'm not stupid enough to think I could make that work. Nor would I do something like that to her." Heath laughed, bringing a smile to his own face. "I'd like to marry her as soon as possible. But I think we'll have to wait until this is all done. However, I do believe Rogen has taken care that we're officially wed in the books downtown. That way, if anything ever happened to me, she'll get any benefits I have for her."

"You know what she does for a living, don't you? I mean, other than the pictures she takes. Which are good." Jonas told him that he thought them beautiful. And yes, he did know what her other job entailed. "Thank you for that. Since their mom passed away when they were just little girls, I've been watching over them. Ginger never gave me a moment's trouble, not in all her life. Sissy…well, I didn't want her marrying that idiot, but she wanted it, and I relented. Every day I wish I'd put my foot down a little harder."

"It wouldn't have done you any good, Dad, and you know it." Ginger kissed her dad on the cheek as she sat down with one of the twin girls in her arms. Marie, he thought she was holding. "I found some pictures that might help you with your search on the building. These have landmarks on them that might help. Also, I took two shots of the mail on the table that have where they were taken. But I'm not sure that it will help either. The building cannot be seen from the sky, I don't think."

Jonas pulled Heath out of the room as the women worked. He had found, over the last few months, that it was easier on a person not to listen to details as they worked. Taking him to the back deck where his father and mother were sitting watching the other children play, he showed him where his house was.

"You all live close, then." Mom sat down next to Dad on the rocker, and Heath sat down where she had been. "I want to apologize about the trouble from earlier. I didn't raise them to be like that."

"You don't have to do that. We have six boys, Heath. I think we've heard and witnessed worse. The boys would take on so about the silliest things." Mom smiled at Jonas when he pulled up another chair. "Jonas here surprised us about Ginger. I'm glad. They're getting along like they've known each other for years rather than only a couple of hours. My goodness, they do make a lovely couple, don't you think?"

"I do. Ginger never was one to get all worked up about a man. She rarely dated when she was in school. Even then, I didn't worry about her. Both girls took self-defense classes when they were younger, and Ginger excelled at it." Jonas laughed when Heath told them how she'd taken down one of the men that had come for them. "My goodness, I was scared out of my mind, and there that little thing was, punching that man like he wasn't twice her size and armed."

"Our boys used to take them classes when they were younger too. But they really didn't need them, not being tigers and all. Now, with Rogen and the other woman working around here, it's been wonderful to learn how to fall and such. Using a gun is something I don't care for, but I have to tell you. I feel a durn sight better about knowing how to use it when the time comes around than not." Dad looked at Mom and kissed her on the cheek. "Maggie, my love here, keeps us all in line, but Rogen and the other women, they keep us on our toes."

"I just bet they do." Heath looked at Jonas then. "Ginger and Sissy will have my estate when I pass on. As I'm sure you know, I'm not a well man. I've had a few scares with my heart, and I'm to take it easy. But I have cancer as well. All over my body, as a matter of fact."

"Ginger told me you've had two surgeries on your heart. I don't think either of them knows about the cancer, do they?" He shook his head. "You'll need to tell them soon, I think. However, while here, I'd really like it if you'd consider having my brother Thatcher look you over. He's a renowned surgeon and might be able to tell you something that your doctors didn't. Or wouldn't." Heath said he'd like that. "I'll talk to him when he gets back. Also, Heath, I wanted you to know that I'm going to talk to Ginger about being changed to a tiger. Not only will she be safer, but she'll heal quicker too. If it comes to that, you might consider it as well. It'll give you a great deal more time and without all the worry and pain with your heart."

"I was thinking that too. I truly was. Thank you for that. Of course, I'll have to talk it over with my daughters. But if they're in agreement that it would help me, I'm thinking it might be just the ticket. Also, since Ginger is staying here with you, I'd like to find me a house to live nearby. The one I had back home, it's just too big for me. I roam around it most of the time, wondering where all the years have gone. I need to start fresh as well, I think." Jonas told him he had three homes right now that he was looking to purchase. "You don't have to do that, Jonas. I can well afford to get myself a home."

"I know that, sir, but it would be my pleasure to do that for you. Especially if it makes Ginger happy. Plus, it'll be nice when we have children that you're here to get to know them." Heath nodded, then lowered his head. "She'll come around, Heath. Even if she takes the kids home with her and makes it work, I do plan on staying in their lives. They'll be my nieces and nephews too."

"That they will. All right. I'll take you up on that. But you don't go overboard in this. I only need a little bit of space." Jonas glanced at his parents when they laughed. That was just what they'd told them when they'd gotten a smaller home. The only difference was, now this one was all on one floor instead of three levels that they'd had. Jonas thought this was going to work out well. Better than he'd thought. He only hoped Sissy came around too.

Chapter 4

It was nearly midnight when Benny found himself a place to get warm enough to sleep. It wasn't that it was all that cold out, but being in the jail had given him a nice warm place to hang out, and without that and the food he'd been getting, he wasn't feeling like he was being done right. Even his house had been locked off from him.

It wasn't like he'd not been warned about hitting Sissy. He had been when he'd popped her the first time. It was her fault both times, too, the way she kept ordering him around about stuff. Like a job. He'd not have married the whiney woman had he figured out beforehand that she wasn't one of them Morgans that had all the money.

The building he was in didn't have anything in the way of blankets laying around. Not that he had expected it to, but it surely would have been nice. Even though there was a great deal of working equipment laying around, he'd not touch that either. He knew better than to fence stuff he'd find at job sites. Those companies went after blood, and he didn't have any to spare. He wished he'd have figured out where Margo had hidden that shit she was always going on about.

Benny had seen it. But when it didn't hit the papers about a new drug out on the market that was killing people, he figured she'd hidden it away better than he could find it. When he got up in the morning, he was going to hunt her down and find out where she'd gone with it. Come to think of it, he thought about how long it had been since he'd been to see her and her kids.

Margo was a flighty thing. She was forever stoned out of her mind on one thing or another too. It had been easy to dupe her about things, like her kids. Not that Benny thought of himself as a pedophile, but to him, fucking was fucking. Especially when Sissy didn't want to put out unless he made her. While that was fun, when she was freed from anything that he'd used to make her have sex, she'd knock him around or find someone that would. Benny didn't count that as knocking her around either. As her husband, it was his God-given right to have her when he wanted. 'Course, she never thought that way.

"Hey, Benny. You in there?" He thought it was Margo yelling for him, but he waited. All he needed to do now was find somebody out there that was pretending to be her to see if he had any money on him. Everybody knew his relationship with his sister. "Benny? Come out and talk to me. I'm hurting real bad, and I can't find none of my kids. That bastard took them again."

Leaning out the second-story window, he saw that it was his sister and that she was alone. "Who took them? Those state people? I'm not messing with them again, Margo. They're meaner than Sissy is when she's in a mood." She told him who it was. "I don't know her. You say her name is JoAnn?"

"Jonas, you fucking shit head. Jonas Robinson. He took them from me when I wasn't home. Even hid them away until I got myself cleaned up. Fuck that shit." Margo let go of a scream that would have woken up the dead had there been any around. "Why am I having to shout at you, dummy? Come out here and talk to me."

He was nearly down the last set of stairs when he was hit from behind. Falling forward, he hit his arms hard enough that he heard one of them crack. His noodle wasn't doing much better. Someone, more than likely the same person that hit him, yanked him up by his hair and dragged him to the middle of the only room that seemed to be devoid of equipment. Margo was brought in the same way and was kneeling before him.

"What did you do?" She was crying then, her face all screwed up in pain and nasty sores. "What did you do to me, Margo? I'm your fucking brother."

"I know that, Benny. I'm hurting really bad now. Really bad. They said that if I told them where you are then—"

Her head just exploded, gone from her shoulders as she slumped over onto the floor. He was covered in her blood and brains when the man across from him said his name.

"Where is it?" Benny couldn't think of what he wanted to know. His sister was dead. Worse yet, she'd given him up too. "Where are my drugs and guns, Benson? Your sister here told us you knew where my shipment was and that you were spending my money. You should know that's going to get you into deep shit."

"I don't know. I've been looking for it myself. I was going to go to you when I found it." His shoulder exploded in pain as the man speaking came out of the shadows and stood in front of him. Someone had shot him, and here he was, trying his best to be cooperative. "Mr. Westbrook? I didn't know it was your shit. I swear it. But I don't know where it's at. As I was telling you,

I've been searching for it myself."

"You have? Not what I've heard about you, Benson. I've heard that you've been taken in and questioned about my items. Do you know how that makes me feel? What it makes me want to do to you?" He looked at his sister, or what was left of her. "Oh, she got off easy. I think, and this is only my personal opinion, she's better off dead than doped up so much that she doesn't know when to shut her mouth. Did you know that her kids had something to do with my items coming up missing? She said you helped them."

"Helped them? No, no. That's not right. If I had known that them kids was in on— You know what? I think I might know where those brats are. My wife, you see, she was wanting me to come and get them from Margo and raise them up as our own. I didn't want to and had to knock her around a bit about it, but once she got herself out of the hospital after what I did to her—I did have to knock her around, you see— she might have gone to get them. You can bet that if they're not at my house, she'll know where they are." He asked him why he should believe him. "I'm not that stupid, Mr. Westbrook. I'd not lie to you because I know you'd be able to hunt me down and murder me off like you did my sister."

"I didn't *murder* your sister, Benson. She did that all on her own by fucking with my merchandise.

And when I kill you, it will be because you had the nerve to touch something that didn't belong to you." Benny swallowed three times before he thought his throat could handle spitting out a few words. But Mr. Westbrook spoke first. "You give me your home address, and I'll go in search of them. If they're not there with that lovely wife of yours…. Well, I'm not sure what I might have to do to you to appease my temper. I'm running out of patience here. That merchandise should have been sold by now. But I'm having to hunt people down and make sure they understand that I'm not a happy man. I'm not. You understand that, don't you, Benson?"

"I do. I really do, Mr. Westbrook. But I tell you right now, I didn't touch your things. Not any of them. Didn't even know about the guns until this very minute." He said that someone knew about them. "Yes, I can see that too. It might well have been them kids. They're sneaky little fuckers if you ask me."

"I didn't." Mr. Westbrook walked around him several times. Each time he was behind him, Benny closed his eyes like he did his butt hole when he had to take a really quick dump. "Benson, I really, for the life of me, don't understand why your mother didn't smother you and your sister when the two of you were brought into this world. I don't even know why she kept you inside of her womb when it was obvious that neither of you were going to amount to shit. I tell you, they'll just allow anyone to breed. Don't you agree?"

"Yes, sir. My mom, she wasn't all that bright either. I don't think she could even write her own name." He didn't know why he was making small talk with the man. Benny tended to babble too much when he was nervous—or terrified, just like he was right now. "Would you like for me to go and get the kids for you? I can do that. I will for you."

"No. I have no further use for you. Don't you agree?" Benny tried to think of one way he could be of some use to the other man, but nothing was coming to mind. It could have been the gun being held to the back of his head like it was being burrowed in so it could see what brain matter was in his noddle. "Benson, it's not been any pleasure at all knowing either of you, Whitmans, I'm afraid."

For his last minutes on this earth, Benny tried to think of one good thing he'd done. Just to see if that would be enough to keep him out of the place his mom used to tell them about when they'd been kids. Not a single thought entered his head that didn't have him—

Noises were going on around him. Benny didn't know if it was something Mr. Westbrook was doing or his brain banging around in his noddle. He was shaking so bad he was sure as shit that was making the noise. But as soon as the gun disappeared, he fell to the ground when someone shoved him there and never opened his eyes.

"Benson Whitman. How the hell you have survived all this time without someone putting a bullet in your head is beyond me." He didn't open his eyes to see who the woman was that was speaking. Instead, he just curled himself into a tight ball and put his hand over his mouth after thanking the woman for saving him. "I didn't save you, moron. I'm here to arrest you. I have some questions for you too, but for now, we're going to— Jesus H. Christ. Did you shit yourself, or is that your natural scent you're wearing? Whatever it is, we're going to have to hose you down before you're getting anywhere near one of my vehicles. Agent, take this creatin outside and hose him off. And make sure you get his crack too. I'd think that someone would have shown him how to wipe his ass long before now, but there just isn't as much good parenting going on nowadays."

Benny didn't know what was going on, but his clothing was cut away from him, and he was standing naked in the yard behind the building he was in. When the cold water hit him in the chest, he was sure they were going to kill him by ice. Dancing around in circles like he was being told to do, he saw the woman coming out of the building with three other men. They were carrying a black bag. He knew what that was for.

Knowing that this group was higher up on the food chain than the police were, he wondered why they were bothering with him. Benny couldn't remember a time when he'd done something to bring the Feds down on him. Nor did he think Margo was smart enough to figure out how to breathe and think at the same time. Drugs. He blamed it on the drugs she was forever taking.

The woman came to stand in front of him. Trying to hide his puny penis wasn't that hard. Even without the cold, he knew he wasn't all that big. It was why he hit instead of just having sex. Women tended to make fun of him because of his size, and that would piss him off.

She asked him what the hell he was hiding. "If you think I give a shit about what you're hiding under your one finger there, you're stupider than I was told you are. I just don't care. What did you tell Westing?" He asked her who that was. "The man that lit out of here like he was running a race. Arnold Westing."

"His name is Westbrook. I mean, that's what I was told." She asked him who told him that. Benny couldn't remember but said he thought it was Margo. "I think she was the one that introduced me to him too."

"You aren't above throwing anyone under the bus, are you, fuck-tard? You introduced her to him, and he used her as a mule until the drugs took over her mind and made her unreliable. Now, let's start again. Who introduced you to Westing? Which is his name. Westbrook is an alias." He honestly didn't remember. But the shot in his arm, the one that Westbrook, or whatever his name was, had put there, was starting to hurt. So were the bumps and bruises he got when tumbling down the stairs. Telling the woman that, she walked up to him and rammed the gun she had on her right into the wound. Screaming and crying now that she'd made it worse, he begged her to stop. "Now that I have your undivided attention, Benny, you're going to tell me how you met Westing and what you told him while he had you. All of it."

"I don't remember. That's the truth." She asked him if he knew what the truth meant. "Not to lie. I know it. But I don't remember. I think someone a long time ago pointed him out to me, and I went on over and talked to him. He wasn't as big a deal as he is now. He's got all kinds of henchmen working for him. I heard that he pays well too, but he never wanted to hire me." The woman asked him what he'd told him. "The kids. I told him I didn't know where they were but that I thought Sissy might have them. She had a real hard-on for them kids. I had to knock her around a little to have her see my way of—"

"You hit her once. Don't fucking lie to me again.

Did you tell him where you live?" Benny told her
Westbrook already knew that. Benny used to stash stuff
for him when he needed him to. Which was another
lie. He'd told him not only where he lived but that
the house was locked up tightly. He let it go for now.
"And in exchange for you stashing shit for him, what
did he do for you? I know you well enough by now
to know you don't do shit without something coming
your way."

"He'd pay me cash so I'd have some walking
around money. Sissy, she's my wife, she never let me
have any cash. No credit cards either. She said we didn't
have money, so I wasn't to get credit. No matter what
I told her about credit not being real money, she'd not
let me." The woman laughed. "I don't think a woman
should be able to do that to a man she's married to. It's
my right by the law of the Bible that I should be the
head of the household."

"It also says you shouldn't kill. I'm assuming
you only pull out the parts you like rather than live by
the rule of the big book." He hadn't any idea what she
was talking about, so he kept his mouth shut. "You're
under arrest. Under Federal law."

As he was told what few rights he had, the
woman walked away from him. There were other
black bags brought out of the building, but he knew
now that none of them were Westbrook—or whatever

the hell his name was. Just as he was being loaded into the ambulance, his ass hanging out there for anyone to view, he felt a sharp pain in his head. Falling back, he thought the woman had killed him anyway.

~*~

Sissy was having no fun at all. The kids were driving her crazy and wouldn't follow even the simplest of orders that she gave them. If they would just do as they were told, they'd not have to go to bed without their supper. Now they were whining about how hungry they were.

Well, not whining. She was doing that. They were in their room. She'd put them to bed at six last night, but tonight it had been four. Sissy just needed some quiet time all to herself, and having four people around, even little ones was making her insane.

The little phone by her bedside rang, and she wanted to scream. It had to be Mrs. Apple again.

"What is it you want now? They're not making a bit of noise. Not that they ever do. And I didn't mess up your kitchen making them supper. They've gone to bed without again." She heard the breathing and thought about who it might be. "Hello?"

"Sissy, have you really put those children to bed at four in the afternoon? Without supper? You said again. How many times have they missed their supper?" She nearly sobbed to her dad when he finally spoke. "What are you doing to them? They've had enough trauma in their lives without someone that is supposed to care for them making it worse."

"They're fine. But since you didn't ask how I'm doing, I'll tell you anyway. I'm not asking you for help or anything, but I could certainly use a break from them, like an entire week. All day long, I'm carting them up and down the stairs to take them to this appointment or something. And that little one. My god, Dad, all she does is pee in her diaper or poop, which is disgusting, then looks at me with those blue eyes like it's my fault I forgot to pick up wiper things. Someone needs to come here, Dad, before my head explodes." Dad pointed out to her that she'd only had them for two days. "So? I'm sure there are hundreds of women that would feel the same way I do if they had to go through what I am. It's all day too. I finally had to make Thomas carry Billy up and down the stairs for me. I have to take that baby out all the time to get what's required to care for her."

"His name is Bobby, not Billy." She rolled her eyes, then asked him if it really mattered what his name was. "I'm sure it does to him. I know it would to me if you were forever calling me the wrong name. Sissy, you must let them out of their rooms and allow them some supper. I'll come and get you and all of them and take you someplace."

"Oh, Dad. It would be wonderful to have dinner

with you. A nice glass of wine. A fine steak. Yes, I'd—"
He told her he didn't believe the kids would enjoy a
steak dinner. "I don't want them with us. I just want to
be out on the town with you. They can…I don't know,
stay here. Lord knows they like being together all the
time."

"I can't believe you're saying this, Sissy. Nor
can I believe I have to remind you of this. They're just
children." She said they were a pain in the ass. "You
just told me they weren't making any messes and that
they were quiet in their rooms. That doesn't sound like
they're a pain. Why don't you allow them to go into
the sitting room? Watch a little television for a change.
Order them a pizza or something for dinner. They can't
go without, Sissy. That's not the way to raise healthy
children."

"Of course, you would take Ginger's side in all
this." He asked her what she was talking about. "Pizza
isn't good for them, and television will rot their already
damaged minds. She put you up to this, didn't she?
Ginger did this. Told you to call here and find out what
is going on with them. Well, they're not dead, nor are
they going to starve to death missing a few meals."

"A few meals? How many have you kept from
them, daughter? What are you doing to those poor
children? As for your sister, I've not seen her in a
few days. She and the other Robinson women are

out working." Sissy asked him if she told him to say that. "What is the matter with you lately? It seems like you're ready to jump on every little thing and make something out of it. I'm coming there now to pick those poor children up. If you're not going to care for them properly, then someone has to do it. You'll have them ready, Sissy, or so help me I'm going to call the police on you. This is not the way to raise children you insisted on having."

"I want you to take me out, not them. I'm sure that living with Margo, they are used to missing a few meals, Dad. Just let me tell them I'm going out again, and I'll be —"

"Again? Again? How many times have you left them there all on their own? Christ, Sissy. You're supposed to be taking care of them. Not stepping out when it gets to be too much for you." She heard him grumbling about how the kids needed adult supervision all the time. "I'm on my way."

Sissy went to her closet to find herself something to wear. Damn the kids. She wasn't sure now why she'd even bothered with wanting them. They were cute, yes, especially the baby. But it was far too much work for her to want to raise all four of them at one time. She was going to tell her dad that too.

While getting dressed, she thought about what she'd said to her dad. They weren't a lot of work.

None at all. Thomas had taken over making sure they were bathed and had their teeth brushed when it was bedtime. Hailey — she didn't care for the way the little girl looked at her like she was plotting — took care that Sarah was in a clean diaper. Sissy really wasn't sure why she was having such a hard time being around them. If anyone had asked her, she'd not even be able to think of one thing that made her send them to bed without their supper.

Dad showed up about ten minutes after she was finally feeling like a new woman. Her hair was brushed and put up in a nice bun. The dress she had on was a little tight, but it wasn't really that bad. However, instead of giving her a hug and a kiss on her cheek as he normally did, he brushed right past her and up the stairs. Following him to see what he was doing, she stopped at the top to watch him talking to Thomas.

"You get yourself cleaned up and dressed, son, and we'll go have some dinner." Thomas glanced in her direction. If he expected her to tell him it was all right, he was going to be sorely disappointed. Instead, she told him to get back in bed. "You listen to me, Thomas. Go on now. I'll take you and the others for some food, and we'll have a good time."

"Do we have to come back here? We've been really good like Mr. Jonas asked us to be. Even taking care that we didn't get under foot. But we're hungry,

Mr. Heath. Sarah's not had a bottle for days now." Dad knew it had only been two days, but to a child, it would seem like forever. He looked at Sissy, and she told him her opinion of the bottle. "She's too little to drink out of a glass. I tried to make it work, but then that woman over there got mad at her when she spilled it on her clothes. Please don't make us have to come back here with her. She's not a nice person at all."

"I am too. Get back in there right now." Dad told the little snitch to get his brother and sisters, and they'd be on their way. When Thomas went to the other three rooms, she looked at her dad. "What are you doing to me? How will I ever make them behave for me if you're going over my head? Dad, I have this under control."

"Do you? He called you that woman. That woman, Sissy. As if he didn't want to even say your name. That isn't a way to have children love you." Sissy told her dad that she'd make them love her. "Can you hear yourself? You can't make anyone love you. Especially children. My heavens, this is a part of you that I'm not proud of. I had a feeling you were having a rough time of it, but I can see I was wrong. Those children are the ones suffering because you want to have something that isn't right for you. A family is loving and works together. They need hugs and food in their bellies. Someone to nurture them when they need it. Have fun with them. You've done none of those things with them. Only alienated them to you."

When her dad left, leaving her there all on her own, Sissy sat down on the bed and looked around at the mess she'd made getting ready for dinner with the only man she'd ever loved. Her dad had hurt her tonight. And he'd taken her family away from her too.

Deciding to get out of the inn for a couple of hours, she made her way down the stairs. Just as she was stepping onto the landing that led her to the front door, her shoe slipped off her foot, and she went tumbling down the rest of the flight.

Every step she hit seemed to jar something loose in her body. Sissy felt her arm crack against the railing. Her head hit the wall. Each time she flipped over, something else would bang against her in some way. Landing at the bottom of the stairs, her head spinning, she looked up to see someone standing over her.

"I fell." It was Mrs. Apple. "I'm going to sue you for this. You should know better than to have things on the steps that will hurt people."

"Well, if you ain't the worse…I'm calling you an ambulance. Not that I think they will help you if you're not any nicer to them than you are me. But I'll call them. Your sister too." She told her not to call her sister. She wasn't anyone that she wanted around her. "Too bad. I'm calling her. You should work on your disposition, young lady. You're about the nastiest person I've ever had in my place, and I'll be happy to see the back of you."

Sissy must have passed out, or that woman hit her. But when she opened her eyes, she saw several people standing over her. Not a one of them was helping her up either. Trying to move, she felt her back twist up, and she closed her eyes once again.

"Sissy. Open your eyes." She tried very hard, but it was too difficult for her. "Sissy. Open your fucking eyes and look at me."

"I hate you." It was Ginger. "You have a terrible mouth too. It's no wonder the kids don't like you. They told me that."

"No, they didn't. Sissy, you're going into surgery in a few minutes. Dad is on his way here. I'm sorry, honey, you've lost the baby." Sissy said that was her fault too. "Yeah? Well, you go on thinking whatever you want. But they're going to operate on you to try and fix your back. You broke it."

"You did this." Suddenly she felt something flow over her. "Ginger, you're not going to take the kids from me. They're mine."

"We'll see. You just do what you're told, and you'll be finished with the surgery before you know it."

Her mind was starting to feel light and fuzzy. Her eyes no longer worked, and she was worried that they were going to poison her before she could tell Ginger to stay away from her.

She opened her eyes again when someone said her name over and over. The man standing over her was telling her that she was going to be put under and that her father and sister were in the waiting room. Sissy couldn't speak, but she did blink several times, hoping he'd understand that she didn't want anyone around when she was out of this place. He didn't seem to understand anything. It would be just like Ginger to get her a half-assed man to operate on her.

As she was falling under the medication, Sissy had a terrible thought. How the hell was she going to be able to go up and down the stairs to take care of the brats if she was indeed hurt? She wouldn't put it past her sister and now her father to make her look foolish, and there was nothing wrong with her other than Ginger was going to take the kids from her.

Chapter 5

"Three men are in the hospital right now, and Benny is dead. I can't think what might have gone wrong with this. It was the perfect setup, as far as I can see, to catch all the men in the operation about the guns and drugs. Did Westing come back? Did he leave a man behind to take care of him? I haven't any idea. The place was covered. I had my best men on the job." Tru paced the big room while telling Rogen what had happened at the building. Ginger was only paying about half the attention she thought she was supposed to be doing. "I swear to you, we took every precaution."

"I believe you. I'm sure Ginger does as well." Ginger nodded but didn't move from the computer she was working on. "What I don't understand, and I'm sure I should, is why there was so much bullshit going on in that building in the first place. I mean, how did he track him there? Where does Margo fit into this? I'm thinking she sold her brother out just to get some kind of a promise of a fix from Westing. Or a payoff. Either way, she should have known she was about to die."

"I doubt it. According to the report I just got back, she didn't have all that much longer to live anyway. Her liver was shot, and she was dealing with other organ failure as well. Malnutrition, as well as a plethora of other ailments that come with being a doper for so long." Ginger found the coordinates she was looking for and narrowed the search down to one-fifth of the area she'd been looking for as the other three talked about Margo. "What the hell are you looking for?"

"The building. I've been able to find the area I was in by the stamp on the back of the photo I took. I wish I'd taken better care to mark it on my map, but I did pull up the envelopes again and found that the address it was sent from doesn't exist. However, the post office stamp was a little more helpful. It came from DC." Enlarging the area that she was looking in, she felt the others standing behind her. "The return address is from DC too, but it's not a real place. The streets are wrong, as in instead of West Avenue, there is only a North Avenue. I know that sounds like a mistake on the addressees part, but I checked, and the only thing on North Avenue with that set of numbers is a vacant lot that hasn't had anything there for the last two decades."

"This building, what do you suppose you'll find once you locate it?"

Ginger told Allie that they were going to send in a group to check it out. Rogen took over the explanation from there.

"The area she was in was a legitimate place where she was supposed to take pictures. The animals were there, but the building shouldn't have been. The fact that it had bodies within a short distance from the front door concerns me on what it is they're doing out there. Drug testing? Human test dummies for some kind of weaponry? I don't know. And I've not asked my boss. There is something very higher up about this that has me worried." Allie asked her what she thought it was. "To be honest with you, I have no idea. The way that the bodies are cut up, the way they're harvesting some things on them and not others. I hate to say this, but it's almost as if they're taking the prime parts from them and leaving the rest. However, that doesn't explain why some are missing lungs and hearts while some aren't. And the way they're getting rid of the bodies is very strange. A mass grave is sort of out there."

"I found it." Ginger moved the mouse to circle the building. "It's difficult to make out right now, but you can see that the ground around it is browning up with leaves, while the camouflage they're using to cover the building is still green. I'm sure that soon someone is going to realize their mistake and change it out. That's what I'm hoping for. Someone to order enough brown cover to make sure it's still out of sight."

"Hot damn, I have it." They all turned to Rogue when she laughed. "Someone just put in an order for fifty-thousand feet of brown camo, as well as snow camo. I wonder if they realize there is no chance in hell they're going to need snow camo. Anyway, I'm backtracking now to see who is ordering it."

As she worked on that, Ginger thought about what her father had said when he'd gone to get the kids. Sissy had been keeping them under lock and key for the last two nights. Also, he'd found out that they got breakfast at the inn, but there was no lunch. Sissy had tried to make them something on the first day and had made such a mess of the kitchen that Mrs. Apple had ordered her to clean it up. The kids had ended up doing that as well. Then there was the accusations that her sister was making about her. How she was making it so that she —

"Are you all right?" Ginger nodded at Rogen. "Don't let it bother you about the kids, Gin. Your dad is having a good time with them, and they're getting a good meal. Jonas is going there to pick them up when they're done and bring them back here for you to cuddle and love on."

"I feel like I've failed them in some way." Allie said she felt like that on a daily basis since becoming a mom. "I suppose all parents do. Dad was so upset when he left here. I thought for sure he was going to beat my sister when he got there. I don't understand her anymore. She was never like this before. How much longer will she be in surgery, do you think?"

"Thatcher said it would be at least another hour. Not only did she break her back, but her ankle is shattered as well. Mrs. Apple said that Sissy was — is that her real name?" Ginger laughed and said it was Cecilia. "All right. Then why Sissy?"

"The kids at the preschool couldn't say it. Cecilia had always been my sissy when we were together at home, so they started calling her that as well. It stuck. I personally think she's outgrown the name, but I can't get her to change it to her real name. Ginger isn't my first name either. It's Brooke. But my mom's name was Brooke too, so I was called Ginger." They all asked her if she wanted to be called Brooke. "I don't care. I suppose if you want, but don't be offended if I don't answer right away. I forget it's my name too at times."

Rogen put up her hand, and they all waited. She'd been giving them all updates on the things that were going on in the operating room. Holding her breath, Ginger wondered what kind of prognosis her sister was going to have when Rogen looked at her.

"I'm so sorry, Brooke, but her spine isn't repairable. When she took the tumble down the stairs, she hit it so many times that her spine was severed in several places. Thatcher said he'd talk to you when he got back, but they're awaiting her head CT to come back now. She hit her head again too." Sissy had already lost the baby, and if she was going to be in a wheelchair for the rest of her life, Ginger…Brooke didn't know how she'd take that.

Looking at the monitor again to give herself time, Brooke thought of the long conversation she and Jonas had had last night. They were going to adopt the children as soon as they could, and then they were going to make sure they were getting all the help they needed. The money that the government gave them—fifty-thousand dollars each for the drugs and another seventy-five-grand for the guns—was going to be put in an account for them to use for college, just as they'd wanted. Her dad was going to match it for them to make sure they never had to work while trying to improve their lives with a higher education.

They were even going to help her sister in her recovery. When Jonas had left her earlier today, taking her dad to find him a home nearby, he'd told her that Sissy was going to need some help. Not just now that she'd been hurt so badly, but with finances as well. The house that she had owned with Benny was being held, as was her checking account. Rogen had told her that it was because of the drug money and the other things they were finding out about Benny and his sister.

"Lately, it seems as if I ask you this a great deal, but are you all right?" Turning to look at Jonas, she smiled at him. "I just heard about Sissy. I'm so sorry."

"I don't know what to think about it right now. I do know, I'm glad we're going to help her. No matter what sort of things she blames me for." Jonas picked her up out of the chair she was in and put her on his lap. "This is where I needed to be all day. How did the house closing go with Dad gone?"

"Very well. He put his other house on the market this morning and sold it within the hour. He said there was a great need for large antebellum houses like the one you grew up in. And he got more than the asking price too." Ginger told him how they were going to start calling her Brooke as she thought about the home she'd grown up in. When Jonas stiffened a little, she knew something else had gone wrong.

"Tell me." He nodded but took her hand into his and kissed the back of it. "My dad or Sissy? Just tell me what is happening."

"When your sister was knocked down at her home, she hit her head on something hard. While the

Kathi S. Barton

hospital there had taken X-rays, Thatcher said they must not have gone over them a second time. She has a hairline crack that goes from temple to temple around her skull." She nodded, knowing there was much more. "Her brain was swollen, pressing up against her eyes as well as her temporal lobe. Thatcher said they're going to have to cut away a part of her skull to let the swelling expand enough so she can heal. I'm so sorry, honey. He also thinks this might be the reason for the sudden change in her. The pressure has been building up for some time now."

"Christ." Jonas held her while she thought about what he was telling her. "Does my dad know yet?"

"No. Thatcher said he'd speak to you both when he was finished up. He thought you knowing now will help with your dad finding out. He seems to think it might be easier on him if you had a heads up."

"Yes, of course." She leaned on Jonas in more ways than one. Her back to his chest and her dependence on him as her mate was all that was keeping her from rushing to the hospital to see what she could do for Sissy. "Let's go and find the kids. Hang out with them and see about getting their rooms set up now that we have them. Rogen filed the paperwork today for them to be ours. I hope that's all right."

"It's better than just all right. I'm happy as I can be about it." As they were moving to the upper floor, she heard the kids coming into the house. Thomas was telling someone about how much pizza he'd eaten, and Hailey was talking about how she'd drank some water without having it in a bottle. "There you are. I was beginning to think your grandpa here kidnapped you or something."

The kids looked at Jonas, then at her dad. "Are you really our grandpa, Mr. Heath?" Dad got down on his knees and hugged Bobby to him, telling the four of them that it was his greatest honor to be their grandpa. "Are we gonna get hugs from you a lot? I have to tell you, I think that'll be the best thing ever for us. I sure did miss them, Grandpa."

Dad was trying his best to be stoic about the kids calling him Grandpa, but he finally broke down. He looked like he'd been given a great gift today and was happier than she'd ever seen him. Brooke — as she was trying to think of herself — hugged the kids and her dad as well. She didn't want to tell him about Sissy just now.

Jonas was telling her dad about the house closing as she took the kids to the kitchen. They weren't hungry, but she did manage to get them cleaned up a little better, and Sarah's diaper and clothing changed. She was going to have to get her more little dresses, as she looked adorable in them.

Dad joined them on their trip to town. There was

little they could do at the hospital, and Thatcher was keeping Jonas informed about anything that came up. To think that a hard blow to the head could change a person so dramatically you didn't know them was astounding to her. Besides, she didn't want the children upset any more than she did her dad. He had been spitting mad when he'd gone after them today.

Getting warmer clothing for the children was a great deal easier than she thought it would have been. They weren't at all picky but excited to have a warm coat that had only ever belonged to them. Gloves too that matched their coats. There were boots to be gotten, as well as pants and shirts. Dad got them each a sled and promised them they'd play in the snow as much as they wanted.

"Did your father talk to you about changing him?" She told Jonas he'd mentioned it, but she hadn't had any time to speak to him since. "He's not getting any better, and making these promises to the kids, I think he's hoping you'll see it in your heart to help him make good on them."

"Really?" She kept an eye on her dad after that. He was making outrageous promises, silly ones, along with ones that were long-off in the future. "I don't have an issue with him being changed. If you do it while this is all going on with Sissy, perhaps it'll be the perfect time for him to not worry about her so much.

I'm going to talk to him tonight about her and what's happened."

"I think he knows it's bad." She had already figured that out. The way he'd be teary when he thought no one was looking. "If you'd like, I'll tell him. With Thatcher in my ear, I can answer as many questions as he might have."

"Thank you. I'll be there, but you doing it will make it so I can hold him if I need it." She knew she was going to need it too. Seeing her dad break down, it was going to hurt her in ways she didn't want to think about.

~*~

Jonas made a couple of phone calls as he was waiting on Hailey and Brooke in the changing room. Bobby had long since gone home with his grandpa, and because Thomas looked about as exhausted as his brother did, he sent him along too. Now it was just him and Sarah sitting on a bench. Shifting her heavily asleep body to his other shoulder, he reached out to Rogen so he could pull out the notes he'd made. If anyone could find out the information he needed, it would be her.

How is everyone holding up? Jonas told her what they'd decided to do with her dad. *More than likely the best thing for now. Thatcher told me she's going to need constant care. She'll likely end up in a nursing home that can care for her needs. Anyway, what can I do you for? Before I forget again, several letters came here addressed to you. I've had them checked, and there isn't much in them but people wanting you to —*

There is a man I think is following us around. That shut her up. She asked him where he was. *Inside Kohls by the ladies' dressing room. If he works for you, he's not very good if I can notice him.*

If he worked for me, you'd better not be able to see him. What is he wearing? After telling her what he was wearing and how he'd changed twice now from a coat to a jacket, then put on a ball cap, she found him. *Okay, I'm going to do a search for him in the face program. In the meantime, you're going to have a couple of men make their way to you. Don't engage, Jonas. I can see you have the baby there.*

I won't. Also, you should know that he's been following us since before we came to the shopping center. I think. I've not told Gin — Brooke, but I think she's aware of him as well. She has sent the boys home with their grandda. Can you send someone there as well? She said she was doing that now. *Thank you for this. I'm not sure what he wants, but I just don't want to have to deal with this now.* He looked at the stands in front of him and saw Tru. *Did you send Tru here?*

She was there already. Something about getting some shit for a dinner. I don't know. She's like me. Close-mouthed. He didn't think any of the women were close-mouthed when they had plenty to say, but Tru hugged him, and he felt the gun she put in the back of his pants. She also took the baby from him. *She's going to take Sarah to someone you can trust, so she's not hurt. Also, Tru will arm Brooke and have Hailey follow her out.*

Then Rogen started cursing. Fluently and loudly in his head.

I'm assuming you've found out who the man is. She said he wasn't going to like it. *More than likely not any more than I do being followed. Who is he, and what do you think he's doing following us around?*

It's a flunky of Westing's. He's there to snatch the kids. Just do what I tell you, and this will be done today without much in the way of bloodshed. He asked her if he would shed any. *Not if you do exactly what I tell you when I tell you. Jonas, you get hurt, and I'll hurt you worse. Your mother will then have a crack at you.*

I understand. I might be a numbers guy, but I know enough to hang onto my own ass when it's necessary. Tru disappeared into the fitting room, then came out with Brooke and Hailey following her to the front of the store. They were told to just act natural and to pay for their things like they would normally have done. *This was fun up until about four minutes ago. Way to rain on our parade, Rogen.*

He was kidding, and she apparently caught that. Telling him that he'd called her first made them both laugh. It was exactly what he needed to make himself feel less stressed.

As they were headed out the door toward their car, the man jerked Brooke from him and put a gun to her belly.

"Do what I say, and no one gets hurt." Jonas didn't even look at Tru as she walked up behind the man and put her gun to his head. "What the fuck? You're supposed to be easy."

"Not so much, as you can see. Let go of my wife, and we'll talk reasonably before my sister there kills you." He asked if he meant to let go so she wouldn't kill him. "No. I'm reasonably sure you're going to be a dead man. If she doesn't kill you, I will. Now, let Brooke go and tell us what the fuck you're doing here."

He'd never been one to use compulsion and was glad that it worked. The man, whoever he was, tried hard to resist him, but in the end, he not only spilled what he knew but more than they thought he would.

"I'm to get the kids. Barring that, I'm to take one of you so you'll turn them over." He let Brooke go, and she turned around and punched the man in the face. "Christ. This is going nothing like I was told."

"Who sent you?" He looked up at Tru when she smiled at him. "I'm not going to ask you again, moron. Who sent you?"

"Westing. He's going to fucking kill me. I hope

you know that." Tru said he had nothing to worry about. "You going to give me some protection for telling you what I know?"

"No. I'm going to kill you before he gets the chance. Where is Westing?" The man said he didn't know at the moment. "Then how were you to contact him when this job went south? You should have known you'd not be able to touch the kids as long as they're with us."

He searched the man for weapons and found, in addition to the gun he'd held on Brooke, two more, as well as a vial and syringe of some kind of clear liquid. He told him it was heroin, enough to kill an elephant. The cell phone was ringing when he pulled it from his jacket pocket.

After making him answer it, Dale, his name, put it on speaker and said the job was done. That he had not just the boys, but the wife as well. Tru was feeding him the information he was to say in his other ear. Westing, he thought, on the other end told him to bring them to the house.

"I'll do that right now." Westing told him they'd better not be hurt. "No. They came along with me easily, just as you said they would. That man, Jonas, he didn't even put up a fight when I took his missus from him."

"Good to know that one thing is going right."

Westing laughed, then spoke again. "If the wife gives you any trouble, kill her. I don't need her so much as I need those brats. When I get them here, they're going to regret ever fucking with my merchandise. I tell you, Dale, no one has respect for the working man anymore. None at all."

When the connection was closed, Tru took the syringe from him and shoved it into Dale's throat. He was dead before she was finished injecting him with it. Leaving his body where it lay, they were headed to the car she'd come in when he saw three men get out of a van and pick Dale up and toss him into the back of it. Christ, he never wanted to get on any of the women's bad side. Not even in a joking manner, he thought.

The drive to the house was punctuated by Tru telling them what was going on in short bursts of information. There were patrols there to back her up. And no matter what they saw when she was working, they were to stay in the car. He was all right with that, but Brooke had an objection.

"He was just going to have that fucking man kill me. And take my children. I want to at least confront him." Tru turned to look at Brooke, and she smiled. "That won't work on me. You might be able to stare down men that piss you off, but I have kids. It just won't work."

"I can't, Brooke. I have orders, and they're not

going to work if I have to keep an eye on you and the idiots that think we're just going to let this ride. I love you to pieces, but if you so much as break a nail, seriously, Rogen will have my ass. And I don't know about you, but I kind of like my butt just how it is." Tru smiled again. "I'm good at this. Very good. I'll be in and out in record time. I won't be if I have to babysit your ass too."

"You could have been nicer about this." Tru said she thought she had been. "You need to work on that a little. All right. You do it, but I want to go with you sometime. Or hang out more. I think I could learn a great deal from the three of you."

"Deal."

Tru slipped out of the car and moved toward the sidewalk that ran in front of the house. When she went up to the door of the neighbor's house, she was let in without any trouble. While he didn't see who had let her in, he had a feeling the people that owned the house were being well compensated for their trouble.

Less than ten minutes passed before she came back out of the house and headed for the car. Several men—he counted about a dozen of them—moved out of the house too and into Westing's home. They were wearing body armor, as well as head gear that made him think they were the cleanup crew.

Without saying a word, Tru drove them home

and let them off. Brooke stopped before getting out of the car.

"You killed him. Just like that." Tru asked her if she was upset about it. "No. Not at all, but I think whatever you're getting paid, it's not nearly enough. I'm also thinking that should anyone go into that house, they're not going to find a single thing to link him to, not just the guns and drugs, but you either. Right?"

"No. Nothing. The men that went in after Westing was dead will go through the house inch by inch. What they don't understand or haven't any clue if it's related to the things he'd been up to, they're to take it to Rogen. Once she has a look into it, she'll destroy it." She asked about the drugs and guns, what had happened to them. "Destroyed. Everything we do, Brooke, is thorough. We never leave anything to chance if we can help it. To us, this is just another job. But we also know we've not just taken a great deal of drugs off the planet, but weapons as well."

"The money you paid the kids that wasn't from the government at all, was it?" Tru surprised him by answering her truthfully. "Thank you for that. I think they'll use it for good. Not to mention, it will give them a much better outlook on the system."

"You're welcome."

When Tru left them, they stood in the yard and hugged each other. When she pulled away and looked up at him, he could have taken on the world and won in that moment.

"I love you." He kissed her and told her he loved her as well. "Good. I think we should put the kids to bed tonight and fuck each other's brains out." Then she turned and walked away.

He was never going to be able to keep one step ahead of this woman. Jonas wasn't sure he wanted to. Nearly skipping into the house, he was greeted by Thomas and Bobby with their new duds on, what they called their new pants and shirts.

Hailey was showing off her "most beautiful dress in the store" that had her twirling around the room for nearly an hour. Sarah was crawling now, or at least her version of the way to get around, and the kids were as delighted as he'd ever seen them. Who would have thought that he'd only taken them in to keep their mother off the street? Now they were his and Brooke's. Jonas noticed that Heath was enjoying himself with them.

Having a family was a great deal more fun than he'd ever thought it would be. It occurred to him that it wouldn't be perfect like this all the time, but he'd have these memories to sustain him when it wasn't. Not that he thought it would be that bad, but he just didn't care. Reaching out to his own parents, he invited them over for dinner, then the rest of his family. Jonas thought they'd all be there for Heath when he was told about his daughter. That, he wasn't looking forward to at all.

Chapter 6

Heath watched his daughter breathing in and out. Because of the trauma of her being operated on, they had put her on life support. The blood staining the wrap around her head made him sick to his belly, but he held onto her hand and told her things that were going on at home. After today, Jonas and Thatcher were going to change him so he'd have more time with his girls and grandchildren.

"The house is nice. I think you'll like it." He sniffled a little, thinking about how she'd not get to play in his garden with him as they had at home. "The place they found for you to live, honey, is the best there is. And not terribly far from where I'm going to be living. Brooke, what we're all calling her now, said I could see you every day. But Thatch, Jonas's dad, said I shouldn't do that. It will wear me out faster than having the grandkids around me all the time."

He thought of the time he'd had with the boys last night. They were all grown men, the Robinsons, but since that was what their parents called them, it sort of stuck. They'd taken him out to dinner—a boys' night out, they'd called it. He hadn't been sure he wanted to go, not with his daughter here, but they'd bullied him into it, and he'd had a wonderful time.

"Hailey is loving school. And I've never seen a little girl want to be dressed up like she does. I think she might have you beat in that department. When you were little, you used to mark your dresses for the month, so you'd not wear the same one twice. Brooke is a good mom with them. She doesn't have a problem at all with making them mind her." Heath laughed. "However, I think it breaks her heart more than it does theirs when it comes to that."

Heath looked at the equipment keeping Sissy alive. There was nothing in here that he knew the name of, but he was sure, should he ask Thatcher or Dawson, they'd be able to tell him not just what it did but how it worked. The men were smart and were making sure that Sissy wasn't in any pain, as well as keeping her quiet until it was time to wake her again.

"That man, Benny. He did this to you, honey. And then the hospital not taking care that you were all right when you left. Rogen is looking into what happened, but she told me she'd take care of them for us." Heath laughed a little. "Now there is a woman that gets the job done. And I'm betting any amount of money that when she says she'll take care of it, you don't need to ask her if she did what she said. Not that I would. I'd be afraid she'd tell me, and she, along with the rest of the women in that family, is not going to hold back a bit on what she'd done to them."

A nurse came into the room, and he backed out of her way. They were armed here. The staff all carried guns and were very showy about it. He knew why — this clinic was where people came that didn't want the world to know why they were there. Thatcher had put Sissy in this part of the building because she was his family.

After the nurse left, not telling him anything, he went back to holding Sissy's hand.

"I won't be around for a few days, baby girl. I've been talking to the family, and I'm going to be changed into a tiger today." He thought about how much pain he was going to be in at first and decided not to mention that to her. "I should be going anyway. Thomas and I have an outing this afternoon. He's going to show this old man how to work on the computer a little. He's a good kid. All of them are."

As he made his way out of the building by the back end, he was struck by how the place was so quiet. Heath knew that all hospitals strived for a level of quietness, but this was more than that. Not a whisper of shoes on the floor when they walked around. No one talking on the phone. It occurred to him that there hadn't been a phone in Sissy's room. No television either that he'd seen. The nurse at the desk made no bones about the fact that she was carrying too. Her weapon was laying right there beside her as she watched the monitors in front of her. They were all friendly to him. But he had no doubt that if it was necessary, they'd blow his head off without a second's hesitation.

When the elevator opened, Heath screamed when Jonas came out in front of him.

"I'm sorry, Heath. Are you all right?" He said he'd been thinking, and it scared him a little. "I hope it wasn't me. I just got off the phone with your banker, and I came by to tell you that all the money in your account has been moved to the one here in town. Also, Sissy's things have been packed up and moved into the garage, as you asked."

"Thank you. I don't know what she'll want done, but I don't want to do anything that will upset her now." Jonas rode down in the elevator with him to the lowest level. "I was going to ask you if you wanted to have lunch with me, but I don't know how much I'd eat. I'm a tad on the nervous side if you want to know the truth of it."

"I think I would be too. But you're going to be all right, during and after. Dawson said he'd give you a little something to calm you down before we start, so that should help you a great deal." They'd told him that, of course, but he was happy to hear they'd not forgotten. "Also, the kids know, and they're having a little party for you before you leave. I think they need it more than you will. They're nervous too, thinking about how much they'll miss you."

"I've never been a grandda before, but I have to tell you, I think I got the best of the crop with them. That Sarah, she just lights up my heart when she grins at me. And Bobby will just sit and hold my hand like we've been doing it for years." Jonas told him they loved him. "They do. They tell me that too. Even Sarah is making the same sounds when they do."

"The other day, they asked me if they could call me Dad. I guess they'd already asked Brooke about calling her Mom, and she cried but told them she'd be honored. I tried my best to be a man about it and not cry, but when I said yes, they hugged me tightly, and that was all it took." Heath nodded and laughed a little. "All right. Our house for cake and ice cream, then off to Thatcher's. You ready for this?"

"I do believe I am. I don't have to tell you to keep an eye on my growing family, but I'm going to do it anyway. You make sure you keep them all safe as you can." Jonas nodded and drove the two of them to his house. "I never would have dreamed this had someone asked me what the future would have coming for me. I have four grandchildren, a great son-in-law, as well as a new start on life. I couldn't be happier right now."

"You remember that when you wake up on the other side of this. Being a tiger will take a lot out of you when you first start out. I know you've been talking to the others about it. Take their advice and do what they tell you, and you'll be just fine." He said he would. "All right. It's a surprise party, so you should act like it, please. They've worked hard on this."

"I will."

When he opened the door to the house, he nearly burst into tears. The big banner across the front hall was something he knew he'd keep for the rest of his life. "Have fun, Grandpa Morgan."

Hugging the kids, he was glad he'd been forewarned about this. He was also glad to see that Brooke was taking pictures of it all that he'd put into an album to look at later. Glad more daily that he'd met this family, Heath enjoyed his afternoon a great deal and was glad for the distraction.

Kissing them all, he made his way to the kitchen where Brooke was with Jonas. They had always been good about that, giving him as much time as he needed or wanted alone with the children. Hugging them both, he walked over to Thatcher's home with Jonas and got ready to change his life. He only hoped nothing went wrong and he'd be in worse shape—

"Don't think like that." He looked at Rogen, who looked in pain. "I don't know what you're thinking, but by the look on your face, I'd say you should never play poker. By the way, I'm going to the hospital to get this kid out, so Thatch is going to take over. You'll be in great hands, so don't let the change bother you either. All right?"

"You're in labor? Now?" She nodded and grabbed the doorway she was standing in and breathed through the contraction. "My goodness, child. We can put this off to some other time. They'll all want to be there for you."

"If they knew. But until the baby is in my arms, I'm not telling anyone. I don't need the added pressure. Thatch only thinks that Thatcher has to go into work. The only other person besides you that knows is Dawson. You're in good hands." Thatcher picked his wife up in his arms and winked at him. "See, we're all in good hands right now."

As they were pulling out of the driveway, Heath shook his head. While they were the greatest family he was happy to be attached to, they were by far the strangest. Going into the room that had been set up for the change, he was quickly laid on the bed and strapped down.

"So you don't hurt yourself or one of our tigers." He nodded. Dawson gave him an injection, and it started working almost immediately. "You're going to be just fine, Heath. Just let it go to work, and you'll be up and around in no time."

After a few more minutes, he was letting sleep take him. His last thought was that he hoped the family had a healthy baby, and he let himself be pulled under.

~*~

"According to the things we found in the house, not only was Westing responsible for the death of Cindy James, but he'd done the killing himself. After a couple of days of beating her to near death, they then took her out into the field where she was found and let the animals have at her. That's the reason for the mutilation on her." Jonas nodded and leaned back in his chair. Allie had all the information he'd need if he wanted it, but he didn't think looking at pictures of what they'd done to the other woman would help him in his sorrow and regret. "Her family has been notified. They've also been given some money to tide them over until they can get back to life. Not that I think they will. Her parents aren't all that much better than Benny's family."

"She told me that. I'd like to make sure she has a nice burial spot, as well as a marker." Allie told him it had been taken care of. "Thank you for that. I'm assuming when you say that you'd rather I didn't get involved with any of this."

"I'd rather you didn't. If they even get a hint that a Robinson is part of this, they'll hound you to death. Not just for more money, but they'll try to get whatever they can out of you. Leave it to rest, and let them do whatever it is they do to grieve." He nodded. "Jonas, you and Brooke haven't bonded yet. I know you've been really busy with all the things going on, but you know she'll be stronger once she is your true mate."

"I know. The other night I'd gotten champagne and roses for her, and one of the kids had a nightmare. It happens less and less now, but they had been so worked up about their grandda having this done that they got themselves in a tizzy. Hailey usually is the one that comforts them when they have one, but it was her this time, and I think the others were at a loss on how to take care of her." Allie told him she could see that. "Is Rogen in labor?"

"Yes. But no one is to know anything about it. She's afraid they'll fuss at her. That's what she said too, fuss at her. So I went out and ordered seven dozen balloons for her, as well as the biggest teddy bear I could find. What do you have planned? Something epic, I'm betting."

"You're not as afraid of her as I think you should be. I'm terrified, so I went low-key." She laughed. "I got her just one dozen balloons, as well as a dozen roses. Also, Brooke got her a basket of things for the baby. Can you believe that for as organized as she is, they'd not put one piece of furniture together yet? What the hell was that all about?"

"She was afraid if she did that, then something would happen to her and the baby. I never realized it until Thatcher told me. And he's afraid of her too." They both laughed. "What is it you want to do with the things we found in Westing's home? Rogen told me it was up to you to sort it out. I would turn it over to the Feds. I can even make that happen for you so that they'd never connect it to us. But there is a great deal of money there, as well as other shit the moron collected."

"Like what?" She handed him a list of things that were in the house. "He was a collector, I guess. What the hell do you suppose he thought that owning a jacket from a singer that died in the seventies was going to do for him?" He handed her back the list as she told him what things were worth. "Okay, I guess he might have been smart about it. I haven't any idea what to think about the house. Is there any use we can find for it? I don't know, donate it to the city for something?"

"Good idea. I think that making it into a gallery

for up-and-coming artists is something we were playing around with before this came up. We could turn it into that, I think." He thought that was an excellent idea. "It has three floors. Maybe we can have a place for kids to come and work on things too. An after-school thing. That would burn his nuts, wouldn't it? To know that children were safe and sound in his home when they weren't when he was alive."

"Yes. I'd like to, if no one objects, name it for Cindy in a way that won't bring her family here." She said she'd think on that. "All right. What else do you have for me? I'm sure when you asked me to come here, it wasn't to slam me about my sex life."

"I've already spoken to Brooke, who I love, by the way, and she said I could tell you too. Mr. Roads, the man that has been calling around for her, is in jail pending trial. He actually used her photo without the markings in a couple of his advertising shots. We think it was a way to get her out in the open when she complained. Whatever his reasons, he's not going to be causing her any trouble from now on. I guess he was going to claim she was a spy, not him like we had thought. Moron." He nodded and asked what had happened. "They were poorly done. It looked as if someone had taken a photo of the photo on a computer and tried to white out the imprint on them. Dumbest and tackiest thing I've ever seen. Then when his computers crashed — she really had embedded her photos with a program to do that — he tried to take her to his offices to fix it. Needless to say, they didn't get far. Brooke had him on the ground in seconds, and the police were all over him in less time than that."

"That must have been what she wanted to talk to me about. I was working with her dad when she contacted me. I'm glad to know she can handle herself, aren't you?" Allie leaned back in the office chair when he sat up. "I need to ask you a favor. I know you can do it, but I need to make sure you want to. The boys want to learn how to defend themselves. Mostly they want to be able to defend their sisters from bullies, but I don't care. I could do it, but I'm worried I'll either be too rough or not rough enough."

"I'd love to do that for them. Also, they should know how to handle a gun. Not that they'll be armed with one, but they should know how to use one and the dangers involved in having one in their hands. Hailey too, if she's willing." Jonas said she wanted it more than the boys did. "Good for her. See? We're good role models for the little girls of this family. You should also have Heath take a couple of classes. It would do him a world of good to know that while his tiger can save him, there are other ways to resolve issues too. I don't think it'll come to that for him, but it would be good that he knew."

"I agree." She asked how he'd done. "Great. The medications he was given made him be in very little pain, and I think he'll be better about this when it's finished too. Dawson said he'd not had too much longer to live. The cancer was starting to eat away at his stomach as well. I'm very glad we were able to do this without any trouble."

Glancing at the clock on the wall, he stood up. Picking up the kids after school was the highlight of his day. Even Sarah was going to some classes so that she could interact nicely with children her own age, but the teacher had told them that she was smart. Thanks wholly, she told them, to having older brothers and a sister. She was also coming out of her shell around strangers.

"Bring the kids by tonight, Jonas. They love our kids." He winked at her. "Yes, I'm setting you up for the night. Don't tell Brooke, however. I think if she knew what we'd talked about, she'd have a kitten. Maybe she'll do that too sometime soon."

Thatcher reached out to them all, and he smiled when his brother was so giddy he could barely contain himself. Waiting for him to gather up his control, Dad told him to get on with it.

We have a daughter. She's beautiful, just like her mom. It was a full five seconds before Dad started whooping it up. *You should see her, guys. Tawny hair, all curly like mine. The cutest little toes and fingers. Come in, but please don't make a fuss at Rogen. She's already lining up hits on you guys should she need to do it.*

Well, you tell her to unline them right now. We're going to fuss, and she'll like it or not, but she will tolerate it. All my grandbabies are going to have a fuss put on them. I don't care who birthed them. Mom asked him how Rogen was doing. *I hope she's not ordering that child around just yet. The poor little thing will need a couple of minutes to know who her mother might be.*

She's doing beautifully, Mom. Nursing Gracie like she's done it a hundred times. And my goodness, the child has an appetite. Dad asked about particulars on the little girl. *Gracie Anne is her name. She weighed in at eleven pounds and four ounces. Full tiger too. She has the greenest eyes I've ever seen. I swear, she's just about the most gorgeous little thing in the world.*

He and Allie were headed into the hospital as Thatcher went on and on about his new daughter. Calling the florist, he finished off the arrangements to have his gifts sent over and then Allie did the same. Beckett refused to go in carrying things so that she'd target her anger at him. Pussy, Allie called him.

"Whatever. You just wait and see how she reacts, and I'm the only one left standing. She said no fuss, and I'm not going to fuss once." They were still teasing him as they pulled into the parking lot of the hospital.

However, Jonas did notice that Beckett had two large subs, along with a gallon of tea that he took in. "She'll need it after having an eleven pound kid. I know I would."

The gifts arrived just as they did. Neither of them helped bring things in. They might be teasing Rogen, but none of them were willing to poke the bear, so to speak. It mattered little, he supposed, when he saw what was already in the room. The president had sent a large vase of flowers, as well as a huge box of things for the baby. Even the FBI had gotten in on the gift-giving and sent over flowers and enough chocolate to feed the county, he thought.

"How did they know you were having the baby and we didn't?" Thatcher explained. "Well, I guess that makes sense. They'd have to know where she was headed and why. But I'm still jealous of all these gifts. I didn't get this much for Christmas in my whole life."

Mom smacked him on the arm when she arrived just in time to hear him complain. After hugging Rogen, then Thatcher, she asked if she could hold the little one. My goodness, Jonas thought, she wasn't a little one at all. All eleven pounds of her looked bigger than he thought Sarah did at nearly nine months.

Mom was a little selfish about holding Gracie, but Dad finally got to have her for a little while. The baby did look smaller in his arms, and he watched as his dad whispered things to her of what they were going to do when she was old enough. He also told her how many cousins she had and not to be worried about hand-me-downs.

"You'll be able to hand them right down too if I don't miss my bet here." Dad kissed her little cheeks and nuzzled her a little. "My goodness, all babies sure do smell good. I'm betting if they could bottle that smell, it'd be worth millions."

"Right up until they crapped their diaper." Rogen reached for her daughter as she laughed with the rest of them. "She really is beautiful, don't you guys think so?"

Beckett leaned over her shoulder and looked at Gracie. "Nah. She's pretty ugly, if you ask me. I mean, look at all that pretty hair, and her skin looks like spun silk. Nope. Just not pretty at all." Rogen smacked him. "Seriously, she very pretty, Rogen. You did good. Perhaps you can have a lot more and make all of us super jealous. Not that I don't already have the market cornered on cute children, but I'll let it pass this one time for you."

The room was filling more than people. Flowers from every government office in the country seemed to have gotten word that the baby had been born. Walking around, he found a basket of fruit from a prime minister, as well as a queen of some country he'd never heard of.

The staff started taking the flowers home with them, whatever they wanted. Even the doctors who had only been on the floor came by to wish the new family well.

When Rogen's brother, Jimmy, showed up to hold his niece, there wasn't a dry eye in the place. He was very careful with her as Rogen told him her name, as well as how much she weighed. Lisha, their mom, was afraid to hold her, so she just held her tiny hand while Jimmy talked to her.

When they were ready to go and get the kids from Mrs. Apple, he was glad he'd taken pictures of the new baby when they asked for them. Sarah even wanted to see her and was touching the screen as if she were playing with one of her little dollies at home.

After dinner, they were headed out again. The kids were going to spend the night at Allie's home. Beckett told him he was excited to be able to have a conversation with children old enough to respond without thinking he was too old to understand things. The younger kids, they thought he was a god. Brooke told him they'd talk his arm off, and he said he had a secret for them. He'd bought a case of different kinds of popcorn they were going to try out. Beckett loved the stuff as much as the kids did.

Jonas had asked Rogen to make them dinner reservations someplace nice. She could get them into anything they wanted without any kind of effort. Not only did she do that for them, but she'd gotten them the honeymoon suite at the nice hotel not far away from where they were having dinner.

Jonas had had flowers delivered, as well as a nice basket of food like sausages and crackers for them to munch on when they were hungry again. Just as he was pulling into the parking lot of the restaurant, his phone rang.

"I just wanted to tell you that everything is paid for. I could have told you earlier, but I was having much too much fun being a new dad. Man, Jonas, this is the best, isn't it? Well, happy wedding night, and have fun. I love you, little brother. When you guys return, I'm going to have a meeting with the people that hired us to look into the newest buildings we acquired. You'll go with me to do the numbers, right?" He said it would be his pleasure, but to leave him the hell alone. "I will. I promise. I do love you, Jonas. All of my brothers mean the world to me."

"Stop being sappy and hang up." They were both laughing when the connection was closed. Jonas looked at Brooke. "He's feeling the effects of being a dad, I think. He's being sentimental. Sappy too."

"He'll get over that quickly, I think. Having to get up in the middle of the night—I'm guessing that will take the sappiness right out of him." He nodded, and they got out of the car. "I'm to understand we're to dress up for this thing? Tru and Allie bought me something to wear. I wonder if I'll like it."

"I'm sure I will. They're very devious, the two of them when they're together." She laughed as they interlocked their fingers and entered the hotel. The man at the desk greeted them as if he knew them and handed Brooke a large bouquet of roses. "This is well beyond what I thought. I love you so much, Brooke."

"And I love you." The valet took them up in the elevator and showed them their room. It was a beautiful suite with vases of roses all around the room. "Oh, Jonas, this is beautiful. Look at the well wishes from people. Look, here's one from the president."

As she looked through the cards and telegrams that had been sent, he looked around as well. The room was very nice. A deep couch was in front of the fireplace, with a throw across the back. Pillows were not just on the couch but on the floor as well. He could see them making love there in front of it.

There were no televisions in the rooms. Nothing to distract them from each other. Not that he thought they'd have that trouble, but it was nice to know that someone had taken their time here and made it perfect. The fridge was stocked, and he pulled out a bottle of water and sipped it. Watching Brooke walk around the room had him thinking about the rest of their lives together.

"I love you, Brooke." She turned and looked at him, and he smiled. "I was just thinking about our lives, how we will be together forever, and my heart took a small bump when I realized I needed to tell you that. I love you with all that I am. With even more than I can express to you in simple words."

"That's the sweetest, most romantic thing anyone has ever said to me." She came to him, wrapping her arms around his neck. "We have dinner reservations in twenty minutes. I propose that we go to eat now, then play around until we make it back here, and you can jump my bones. Does that sound like a good plan to you?"

"Yes. But I'd rather just make love with you. Jumping your bones? Well, it sounds like you're not going to be a participant in this. And I'd really like for you to enjoy it too." She told him she planned on that. "Good. Dinner. Fooling around. Then making love in front of the fireplace, then the bed. And if we're not too exhausted, we'll start all over in front of the fireplace."

"I love the way you think, Mr. Robinson." He kissed her quickly on the mouth, telling her he loved the way she looked. "You're just hoping to get lucky. I will tell you, it's going to happen. Even if I have to work my magic on your body and give myself some fun."

"Get dressed, please. Or we'll never make it."

She turned to go to the bathroom but paused before leaving him there. "What?"

"I have never loved anyone as much as I do you, Jonas. And I can't imagine how much more I'll love you when we're together for the next fifty or so years."

His heart felt full. Jonas didn't think there would ever be a time he could tell her how she made him feel. How she gave him so much with just a glance in his direction. Jonas was in love. Deep and profound love.

Chapter 7

Dinner had been delicious. Romantic too. There had been champagne at the table, as well as a plate of chocolate-covered strawberries. Brooke loved the attention that Jonas was giving her as if she were something precious to him. The pampering wasn't anything she was used to. But Jonas made her feel like she was the only other person in the restaurant besides him.

Back at their hotel room, he looked at her like he was the stalking tiger that he was. Every glance in her direction made her feel warm. Wet too. When his nostrils flared, she felt her body warm more for him. Need blanketed around her and held her tightly.

"That dress is sinful. You've no idea how many times I wanted to rip it off you and lay you out on the table to have as my main course." She giggled at him and slipped her shoes off. "Those heels are killer. The way that slit up the side of the dress shows off your legs. I can only wish that you would wear high heels all the time."

"Not very practical, but I'll give it my best to wear them as much as I can. How about that?" He pulled her into his arms when she was close enough to touch. "You've never worn a suit around me before. I love the way the cut makes you look larger than life. Double breasted is the only thing you should ever wear when you go to meetings. I think from this look alone, you'll win every debate you're up against."

He kissed her then, his mouth hot to the point of warming her from the inside out. When he pulled away from her just enough so they could see each other, she pulled his tie off and began unbuttoning his shirt.

"I've never been undressed as an adult before." Again she giggled and felt good about being the first to do something for him. Telling him to turn around, she finished taking his shirt off, careful of his cufflinks that were as beautiful as he was handsome. "Do I get to remove your clothing too?"

"Yes. If we make it that far." He laughed and turned toward her. His chest was bare to her, and she couldn't help but run her fingers through the fur on his muscles. "You're deceptively muscled, aren't you? I mean, you look like your brothers in being toned, but you're extremely well built. I'm betting it comes natural for you."

"I want to see you now. Show me what is hidden behind your dress." It was a simple thing to untie the small bow at her neck and let the silk creation slip off her shoulders and to the floor. "Christ. You're more beautiful than I could have imagined. And I have imagined a great deal."

Brooke had not worn anything under the dress. Not even panties, as they would have been visible because of the dress being so tight. When she stepped to him, letting him have his fill, Jonas dropped before her and pulled her wet pussy to his mouth.

"Yes." She came twice when he touched off her core. Holding onto anything she could reach, Brooke thought for sure she was going to fall when he spread her legs wider for himself. "Jonas, I'm going to fall."

No, you're not. Just let me have my tastes, and I'll take you to bed. Christ, I've wanted you since the first time I realized who you were to me.

Her body was his. When he commanded her to come, she did so.

When her legs were too weak to hold her up any longer, Jonas helped her move to the bed. Her body was spent. Her arms and hands could no longer hold onto anything. As soon as she was lying on the bed, her body in the middle, Jonas stripped off the rest of his clothing and stood there holding his cock in his hand.

"I'm going to come all over you first. Otherwise, I'm going to take you hard and fast, and I'd hate that for our first time." She said that was the way she wanted it. "You don't. I'm so needy I hurt with it. When I come on you, love. I want you to taste me. Please? I need to watch you take some of me into your mouth and swallow."

Sitting up on the side of the bed, she watched as his hand slid up and down his cock. Her heart rate was so loud she knew he could hear it. Reaching down to his cock, she cupped his balls in her palm and felt his hot cum spray on her face and chest.

Jonas cried out as he came. Holding onto the side of the bed, in a vague sort of way, she knew his cat was right there as well. Deep claw marks scratched into the wood surface, and that made her all the more wet. His cat, right there, made her want to beg to let him go. Instead, he pushed her back on the bed, with her legs hanging over the side, and slammed his cock so deep into her that she felt it at the back of her throat.

He took her hard and quick. The punches of his cock to her body were nothing compared to the climaxes she had, each one like the little death she'd heard them called. Every time she came, Brooke felt the earth move under her, her body take more of her mate deeply inside of her.

When he stilled, Jonas's body poised above hers for a moment, she knew he was coming. As soon as he yelled out her name, the heat of him filled her until she was once again on the verge of coming. And when she did, coming hard enough to shake her to the very core of her life, stars danced around behind her closed eyes before everything within her seemed to just blackout.

Jonas was wrapped around her body when she woke. The sheet was over the both of them, but nothing else. Raising her head just enough to look around, Jonas asked her if she was all right. She had to think about it while she moved around to face him.

"I feel wonderfully sated but woefully sore. How about you?" He said he wasn't sure he would ever be able to have sex again, that she'd broken him. "I hope not. I plan on having you later."

"Only if you want to kill me." They were both laughing when he sat up and moved to the fridge in the room. "I have some food here if you think you've worked off a few calories. It's all I could think about when I woke up a few minutes ago."

"I'm hungry too." When she sat up, her body made it clear there was just too much pain for her to even think about sex again. "I need a warm bath. And a good long nap after we eat. What time is it?"

"Just after four in the morning. I'm thinking I could use a good nap too. You really have broken me."

He sliced some of the cheese and sausage off the roll for her and fed it to her in small bites. She did the same with the grapes and apples that were there.

They talked about nothing really. As soon as he put the tray on the table near the bed, he curled his big body around hers. Talking about the kids, if they wanted to have any more, she told him that waiting would be a good thing for now.

"I agree with you there. However, if you were to get pregnant, what would you like to do?" She wasn't sure what he was asking, so she asked. "I mean, you're not going to make it go away, will you?"

"Never. Not ever. If I were to find myself pregnant with your child—is this your way of telling me that I could very well be pregnant?" Laughing, he told her no. But they'd not discussed having more children. "Anyway, if I were to find myself having your child, nothing would come between me and having it. It would be meant to be. But I would like to wait. For a little while anyway. I'm not sure how well adjusted the kids will be in a year, but I do know that Sarah will be a little less needy of me carrying her everywhere."

"I agree with that. However, Mom told me not to wish for her to be walking quickly. She'll be able to get into things better, as well as higher up. It's like talking, she told me. Once they start, they never shut up."

Closing her eyes, she wondered what it would

be like to have a child with this man. It would be epic. She knew that.

Once she was asleep, the dreams she'd been having the last few days came to the surface. This time they were more vivid, colorful, it seemed. She and Jonas around a large Christmas tree, with a dozen small and big kids there with them. Then, like before, she fell into a deep sleep that had her dreaming of nothing more.

Waking in the big bed alone, she was disappointed. But then she stretched out, pulling muscles that were tender and sore, and decided she was glad for being alone. Hearing the shower running, she made her way there after slipping on Jonas's shirt he'd had on last night. He was whistling, a sound she'd not heard from him before.

When he turned off the shower, she kissed him when he opened the shower door. His body was just too good to resist, and she ran her fingers through the tufts of fur on his chest. When he laughed, she looked up at him.

"As much as I'd like to reciprocate, I'm sore. I have to admit, I've never had sex before where I was just too sore and achy to have it again and again." She told him she was too. "We're going to have to keep it low-key for at least a day or two. I don't want you hurt any more than I want to hurt myself. And I do believe I would. Even getting hard is painful. By the way, you look very fetching in my shirt. That should be your mode of dress for bed from now on."

"I think I will. Usually, when I go to bed, I'm naked, so if you want me dressed, then that's—" Screaming, she ran out of the bathroom when he came after her. Laughing hard when she was tackled to the bed, she told him how much she loved him. "I do, you know. Love you with every fiber of my being."

Touching her fingers to his face, she moved a lock of his hair from his forehead. He kissed her then, gently. There was so much she wanted to say to him, telling him how he was perfect for her. That he'd saved her from a life of loneliness too. Jonas leaned down and kissed her, and Brooke felt like everything that needed to be said was said to each other in that one kiss.

"We have reservations for lunch at one. It's eleven now." He stood up off her and wrapped the towel around him that he'd had in his hand when he chased her. "Christ, you're beautiful. But duty calls. While here, I'm supposed to look at three properties Rogen wants to purchase. Then tomorrow, sadly, when we get home, I'm to go with her to a meeting about some other things she has going on. Dawson might be there as well."

She asked him why it seemed as if he was babbling. He told her. It was babble like a fool or jump her where she laid. Laughing, she sat up on the bed, pulling his shirt around her better.

"To be honest with you, Jonas, I feel like I've been run over about sixty times. After that, someone shoveled me up from the road and put me into a washing machine on full blast. Even my hair is a little sore."

She went into the bathroom to shower. As soon as the stinging water hit her, she knew this was just what her poor body had needed.

They had an enjoyable afternoon and even a great lunch. They didn't buy much for themselves, but they did for the kids. Christmas was coming up in a few months, and she decided if she started now, she'd be finished by Christmas Eve. Jonas told her he was excited to get gifts for all the kids this year.

"It's the family's first Christmas with children surrounding us. Mom and Dad are going to go all out, I'm betting. Dad was complaining to me the other day how Mom was buying things he'd been thinking about getting them. They're even thinking of putting in a nice pool for when the kids come over to their house in the summer." Brooke said she was glad they had one. The kids had seemed to enjoy it up until it was too cold to use it. "Bobby has been wanting to get into it since they moved in and found out that we had one. The kid has missed a great deal this summer with being in casts."

After their lunch and seeing to the houses, both

of them passes as far as Jonas could see, they made their way back to the hotel. Brooke was excited to be going home tomorrow. She missed the kids and her dad. Not that she'd been able to speak to him while they'd been gone, but Dawson had kept her updated on his progress.

On the way home the next day, they talked about how they were going to celebrate being home with their kids.

"We should order some pizzas for the kids for dinner tonight. I've noticed that between the four of them, they could make it a food group all its own." Brooke said she'd noticed that as well. "I miss them. Very much. I know we were only gone for a couple of days, but I have missed putting them to bed and hugging them."

"I was thinking the same thing. Who would have thought only a few weeks ago neither of us had any kids. Now, not only do we have four, but we're happy with them too." Jonas agreed. "Watching them come into their own is going to be fun. I can already see bits of their adult personalities coming around. Can you?"

"Yes. Thomas is going to prove himself, I think. I can see him as an attorney for the underdog. Hailey will be in research. Germs and such that can be put into things that will harm others. It's hard to tell about Sarah." She asked him about Bobby. "Him? Well, I don't know for sure, but Bobby is going to be someone that can be trusted with government secrets and hold them tightly to his chest. Like Rogen. Have you noticed that he hangs out with her more than any of the other aunts?"

"Yes. He's not afraid of her either like the rest of us are." Jonas said that was very noticeable to even Thatcher. "I only want them to be happy. Seriously. If they never leave home, I say this now, then I'd be very content."

They were still laughing about that as they pulled up in front of their home. The kids, all four of them, were there to greet them. Brooke didn't think a better homecoming could be had than this. Children made the world a tolerable place, she thought.

~*~

Being back home now, Jonas felt like he belonged. He knew that he *did* belong here, but there was something about having his life settled that made him feel like he was in charge of his own life. Laughing, he realized he wasn't in charge of anything as soon as Bobby, who was sporting a boot on his leg, came hobbling into his office and sat down.

"I don't like girls. Not one bit." Just catching his laughter, Jonas asked him what had happened. "There is this girl, a yucky girl at my school, that says she's going to marry me. I'm just a kid. How the heck is that even going to happen? It's not, I can tell you that. I don't even like her at all. She is yucky and a girl, Dad. Yuck."

"I see. This girl, do you happen to know if she's a wolf?" He said she was. "Okay, now this is important. Did she say that you were her mate? Like Brooke is to me? Or did she tell you she was just going to marry you? Remember now, she's a wolf, and wording can be important in this."

Bobby thought about it, cocking his head with his eyes closed. "She said I was her mate. Oh, no, Dad. I'm just a kid. I don't want to have to kiss her and stuff. Have I told you that I don't even like girls? You have to fix this for me. Please? I'll do whatever you want. I don't want to be her mate for nothing."

Jonas thought about an eight-year-old being mated, and he had to stop and think about how that was to work for them.

"Who's mates?" Brooke came into the room and sat down on his lap. "Have you found your mate, Bobby? That's wonderful news. You're going to be so happy with her."

"I'm happy now. I don't need some dumb girl to make me happier." Bobby made a couple of gagging sounds and got up to leave. "I think this is dumb and not even going to happen. She'll just have to find herself another mate. Someone that likes girls more than I do.

Which can be anyone so long as it's not me. Double yuck. I think I've been set up like a chess game that I'm going to lose."

When he left them, both he and Brooke started laughing. "I'll contact Shane and see what he knows." She asked him if it was Shane Picket. "It is. Do you know him by chance?"

"I do. He had a couple of things going on a few years ago, and I worked with him taking some pictures. I don't remember what it was for now that I have time to think on it, but I'm sure it's the same one." She snapped her fingers. "His pantry. He has it laid out in a way that not just saves the product in it, but also keeps things at hand when they need them quickly."

"I'm sure it is the same one. And I've seen how he does the food storage. It's amazing. The fact that he also has a shed that handles goods someone might need in the event of a house fire or something is wonderful. His pack is huge now, and they're helping us with a great many things. I'll call him so you can talk to him as well." Picking up the phone, Shane answered on the first ring. He was talking a mile a minute, and it took Jonas a moment to realize that Shane was talking about how Belinda Donaldson was the mate to his son. "So, it's true then. Bobby was just in here talking about how he was mated to some yucky girl."

"She's a good kid. I'm not sure what yucky means

to a kid, but she's beautiful. I'll send you a picture of her." His cell phone dinged, and he and Brooke looked at the gorgeous little girl. "I've never seen this happen with a human and a wolf before, but I'm thrilled by it. This way they can grow up together, and protect each other too. I'm sure that Bobby will soon grow out of thinking he doesn't want a mate."

"No doubt sooner than we think, too." Brooke told him who she was. "I believe you and I worked together on a project for the wolf council about four or five years ago. They liked the way you had set up your food pantry and wanted to make the plans available to every pack. It is you that I worked with, correct?"

"It is. Holy shit, Jonas, you didn't tell me you were married to someone like Ginger. She's a catch. How the hell did you get so lucky?" He said he was lucky, he thought. Then he told him that she went by Brooke now, as it was her first name. "Good for her. How are your sister and Dad, Brooke? I'm betting she has a passel of kids by now."

"Sissy has been hurt, Shane. Badly. She's in the hospital in a medically induced coma." Shane told Brooke that he was sorry. "My dad is here as well. I'm betting he'd love to see you. He only just bought him a house nearby and is having fun with our kids. Bobby will no doubt have plenty to tell him when he talks to him later. They're good at putting their heads together about things."

They spoke for a few minutes more before Brooke's cell phone rang. It was the hospital, she told him as she left him to answer. Shane told him he'd keep an eye on the budding relationship and would tell him what he knew.

"I'll send you updates when I get them. It's kind of fun to be able to watch the two of them as they grow into this. As I'm sure they will eventually." Jonas asked about sex and that sort of thing. "I don't know that they ever feel that as young as this. As I said, I've never seen a human and wolf come together. They'll be protective of each other for sure, which is what you could expect. As for sex? No, I'm sure his body and that of his other half, in this case, Belinda, will tell them when they're ready for it."

When Brooke came back into the room, she looked pale. Hanging up from talking to Shane, he went to her. Holding her in his arms, she nearly collapsed. Picking her up, he took her to the couch in his office, holding her until she was ready to talk.

"My sister died an hour ago. That was Thatcher, who called from the hospital. He said her temperature spiked, and there wasn't anything they could have done for her when she had three strokes within the span of about five minutes." Jonas held Brooke as she sobbed. "I never got to talk to her about anything.

There were so many things I wanted to share with her. Oh, Jonas, I have to tell my dad too. He's going to take it especially hard."

She cried again, and he reached out to his brother. *I was here when she stroked, then coded. Brooke's dad had put in an order for her not to have heroic efforts made, as we weren't sure what her life would be like after the swelling went down.* Jonas asked what had happened. *We were regulating her intake of fluids when they simply stopped. Kidney failure was my first thought. Before I could send her for any kind of X-rays, she stroked the first time. Then a second time, which left her with her brain swelling more. After the third one, there was no brain activity at all, and I made the call. It's the hardest one I've ever had to make. But as soon as she was pulled from life support, she didn't have any activity at all on her brain or heart. I'm so sorry.*

Heath had been visiting her daily before he was changed. Today was his first day back to see her. Was he there when this happened? Thatcher said he was until a little while ago. When Thatcher had come in to see him, Heath told him he couldn't believe how different Sissy looked. Heath had held Sissy's hand while she flatlined. *Christ, this is just horrific. I know you did all you could for her, and I'm very grateful for that, but I think Brooke is mostly upset that she didn't get to see her sister one more time after the argument they had.*

Her personality changed with the brain swelling.

Tell her that. Her sister wasn't her sister, as her brain was swelling up so badly and causing her so much trouble. I'm sure Sissy might not have known things were any different than they were before being hurt. There should have been more care taken when she was in the hospital when she was admitted. Had they done a better job of looking at the X-rays, she might well have been alive right now. As it is, the hospital is being investigated — not my call — but they'll figure out what happened, and this will be thoroughly investigated. Jonas said he would talk to Brooke, but he didn't think it would do much good until she spoke to her dad. *He's on his way home. I sent him home in the limo. I didn't want him driving. Heath isn't taking it as hard as I thought he would, but then he was here daily, seeing the changes to her meds and monitors too. I honestly think he was relieved to know she's not suffering anymore. We, as doctors, have no way of knowing what is going on in a patient's mind when we induce them like we did her. But I'm sure she was hurting in a lot of ways we'll never understand.*

Jonas held Brooke as he told her what Thatcher had told him. There was little to nothing that could have been done for her. And that her dad had been there when it happened. She asked him how he was.

"Thatcher said he was doing well when he left there. He thought that he was slightly relieved to know she was no longer suffering." He went on to explain it the way his brother had. "Heath is on his way here.

Thatcher sent him home in one of the cars so he'd not drive. It might hit him hard once he sees you."

"I'll try to be strong for him, but I have a feeling we're both going to fall apart once we're together. She was so young, Jonas. Not even in her late thirties." Jonas didn't comment. He knew she didn't require him to, so he just held her. "I'm also worried that the kids will have terrible memories of her. Maybe I can get Thatcher or Dawson to talk to them about how she'd been very ill for a long time and wasn't the person they were with that week. Do you think one of them will do that?"

"I do. They'd gladly do that for them." He asked Thatcher if he would, and he said that he was going to suggest it himself. "Thatcher said he'd do it. Talk to them about what had happened to her and how it changed her deep in her mind."

When the front door opened and closed, Brooke went to it. He knew it was her dad as soon as they both starting crying. Getting up, he led them to his office, then closed the door so they could talk. As he was leaving, he heard Brooke telling her dad what he'd told her. He knew they needed time to deal with this.

Hailey came down the stairs as he was standing there.

"What happened?" He told her about her aunt and that she'd passed away. "That's terrible. I didn't like her much, but she was nice when she wanted to be. Do you think we'll have to go to the funeral too?"

"I think Brooke and your grandda would like you to be there for them. A child, even as ornery as you are, is very comforting when there is a death in the family." She laughed and then stopped suddenly. She told him how sorry she was. "You can laugh, Hailey. It's all right to be just a little sad and happy when someone dies."

"I don't know anyone that has died. Well, my mom did, I guess. But I didn't see her." She came to him, and he picked her up in his arms. "I'm glad you took us in, Dad. I don't think any of us would have lived much longer had you not found us. Even Cindy told us how wonderful of a person you are. And now we have a good mom that treats us nice."

"I'm glad to know you're happy, honey."

They ended up in the kitchen, where both Thomas and Bobby were. They were arguing over the snack they wanted. Mel, their new cook, smacked her hand down on the table between them, and that got their attention.

"I'm the cook here. You'll eat what I put before you." They both looked down at their laps as they agreed with her. "Now. I can make you apples and peanut butter and apples and fluff. I'm very good at that."

In the end, the kids shared their snacks with each other, and Sarah was given peas to eat. Jonas laughed at how she had to concentrate so hard on just being able to pick up one of them at a time. Hailey had a peanut butter and chocolate sandwich with apples on the side. He had a bite of everything.

Heath and Brooke joined them a few minutes later and joined the six of them in arguing what was the best snack in the whole world. Mel won. Having a nice fruit salad with creamy sweet dressing was even his favorite.

Chapter 8

Thatcher was exhausted. He knew Dawson was as well. The two of them had been called to another center like theirs to work. Nineteen agents had been shot. Four of those had died at the scene. While they'd not told them what had happened, Rogen told them what she was aware of. So earlier in the day, he'd asked her what the hell had gone down.

"A man they're calling John Doe was apprehended. He had an arsenal at his disposal, and it looks like he used every bit of what he had to keep from being arrested." Thatcher told her what he had on his end. "I would imagine there are even more than that someplace else. Thirty agents to go in isn't nearly what I'd be taking in."

"Three of the ones that were brought here are dead. One more isn't going to make it. There are no name tags on these men and women. How will they know who is who when it's all finished, and they have to contact their loved ones?" She had told him. "I guess I thought they all had families like you and Tru do. Is that why she only goes out on clean-ups that are relatively safe?"

"I would imagine she goes out on assignments that none of us know about. You have to remember that she's clean up, and there are none better than her. Just like me and my computers."

She told him whatever she found out throughout the day, and he relayed the information to Dawson.

The two of them worked well side by side. Dawson had been in ER for so long he was very good at making quick decisions about what he needed to do. Thatcher wasn't that quick, but he was learning to work on the fly, as Dawson was so fond of saying.

Now here they were, in the middle of the night, driving back home. He'd wanted to take a flight back — it would have been easier — but Dawson told him that he just needed to unwind for a little while, and driving the two hours was just what he would need. When they pulled into an all-night diner, he looked at his brother.

"I'm starving. I'm sure you are, too, if your stomach noises are any indication." He said he could eat. "Thatcher, I don't know if anyone has ever pointed this out to you before, but you say that all the time.

Like, is there ever a time when you aren't hungry?"

"Never." They got out of the car and walked up to the quaint little place. "I didn't know this place was open again. I mean, after the previous owner passed on about five years ago, I just thought it would never reopen. Remember coming here after a football game?"

"I didn't play ball. But I do remember coming here with Mom and Dad for breakfast a few times a month. Best grits in the state, I think Dad used to say." The waitress told them to have a seat wherever they wanted, and they opted for the one close to the long bar that had neat little red stools lined up in front of it.

"*Cad a oíche.* What can I get the two of you?"

Thatcher understood her saying that she'd had a night but didn't comment. Dawson looked at the woman.

"Irish." She shook her head and told him she was Caitlynn, just as her nametag said. "No. I meant you're Irish."

"Aye, that I am. And you be a scholar, aren't you?" She winked at Dawson with a sassy grin. "I've some fresh tea brewing if you've a mind to try it. Also, there is coffee for the heathens that wish that nasty brew."

"Tea. I'm sorry if I insulted you." She said she was having a wee bit of fun with him, and Dawson nodded. They both ordered the tea. "Also, if you have some lemon, I'd like that as well."

"You'll not be messing with my tea with a drip of lemon, I'll have you know. Are you daft, man?"

They both were smiling when she walked away, laughing a lyrical laughter that had him wishing she'd sing to them.

"I'm sappy again." Dawson asked him what it was now, and Thatcher told him about her laughter. "Doesn't it sound like a song we should listen to?"

"You are sappy. What does Rogen do with you when you get like this? I'm betting you run and hide from her, so she doesn't slap you upside the head." Dawson shook his head as he continued. "I feel out of sorts myself. Like something is terribly wrong with—"

The man came out of nowhere. He pulled Dawson from the seat he'd been in and had a gun to his head. Thatcher didn't move, but he did talk to the man, asking him what was wrong and not to kill his brother. Then Caitlynn was there too.

"Da. Stop this. Stop *ag gortu' an fhir seo*, Da?" Caitlynn telling her dad to stop hurting Dawson wasn't working until she shoved her way between them. "Da. It's me. Caitlynn. Your wee bonny lass. Come on now. Don't hurt him. You've been woke up too soon, I can see that."

"What can I do?" Caitlynn told Thatcher there was nothing. That her dad suffered from night terrors and sleepwalking. She cautioned them not to wake him suddenly. "I can't let him hurt either of you, Caitlynn. Get him to stop, or I'm going to have to take him down to the floor."

"Did ya hear that, Da? This man is going to hurt you if you don't wake up and let his poor brother go. Is that what you be hoping for? Come on now, Da. Let the man go and —"

The gun went off, and Thatcher jerked the man off the woman and to the floor. It wasn't until he searched the man for any wounds that he turned to ask Dawson if he was all right. It was Caitlynn that had been shot. Her blood was staining her white shirt like it was going to stain it red before she fell to the floor.

"Oh my God, baby girl. What have I done?"

The man moved out of the way when Dawson told him to. After laying the woman on the floor, Dawson went to work on her. The man, they'd never gotten his name, started sobbing that he'd killed his little girl.

"Go get my bag, Thatcher." He nodded and went to the trunk to pull out both their bags. He was thankful now that they'd been able to get some good supplies while at the other clinic and rushed back into the restaurant. "She's not going to make it. Christ, this is a nightmare. I'm going to change her. It's the only way to save her."

"Are you sure you want to do that?" Dawson looked up at him, and he saw it. "She's your mate."

"Yes. I didn't know until she was standing between me and her father. I have to save her, Thatcher. She's not going to be happy, but I have to do something." The sound of the gun going off in the kitchen had them both pausing. "Go and see what that old fool is up to. I swear to you, Thatcher, I wish now the two of us had taken the plane."

Dawson was shifting to his cat just as Thatcher opened the swinging door to the kitchen. There on the floor, with the gun lying beside him, was the man. He had just finished slitting his right wrist when Thatcher got to him.

Making a decision that would change the course of two people's lives, Thatcher let his cat take him too. Licking the wounds closed at his wrists, he knew he'd have to work fast. There had been a lot of blood loss. The first wrist he'd cut had been too long, and the old man was probably losing his grip on life even as he shot his gun off, Thatcher thought.

Biting into the soft part of the man's belly, Thatcher tore at his flesh so the change would hopefully be quicker. Praying that he could save the man's life, he tasted the chemicals that the man had been taking. Antidepressants. Large doses of caffeine. A cocktail of all kinds of over the counter drugs mixed with the ones that had been prescribed was what was poisoning the man, causing his nightmares, as well as a great many other things Thatcher could taste.

After the man's heart started beating better, his breathing evening out too, Thatcher sat back on his haunches and watched him. Exhaustion like he'd never felt rolled over him in ways he was sure no one on this earth could have been prepared for. Dawson joined him in the kitchen with Caitlynn in his arms. He laid her on the floor beside her father and sat down next to him.

Putting his hand in his fur, Dawson started talking. "We're going to need some help here. I don't mean with getting the two of them home, but there is a lot of blood out there that someone is going to notice. In here, too, it seems. Can you call Rogen?" Nodding, he pulled out his cell phone to call her after shifting to his other self. He was glad to see the blood was gone and that his clothing was intact. "Will you start off with the fact that I found my mate? That might make her less pissed off at me if you do that."

"She won't be mad, Dawson. We did what we had to do." Rogen answered on the first ring. She asked him where the hell he was. "I'm in a sort of a bit of trouble here. Nothing major, but we have a great deal of blood that needs to be cleaned up, as well as two people we've had to change."

"Where are you?" After giving her the name of the place, he told her what had happened. "Well, of course, I'm not going to be mad at him. What a thing to say to me. All right, Thatcher, I'm at the computers. Tell me again the name of the place the two of you are in. By the way, why did you call me on the phone? Usually, you just reach out to me."

"My dad taught us that. When you reach out to someone in the middle of the night, they might not wake fully and incorporate whatever you're saying to them into their dreams. They may or may not remember it in the morning or even wake enough to help you if you need them. So we call first." Rogen said that was a wonderful idea. "Dad has them on occasion. Sometimes they're off the wall, but he is the greatest."

"All right. I have the place. Boy, there is nothing around it for miles. I can have a clean-up crew there in about twenty minutes." He told her he didn't need Tru. They'd only just saved the people. "A clean-up crew to make sure there isn't a trace of blood behind, moron. Christ, I love you. Also, I'll call in some fill-in people to work the place. According to the things I'm reading, for being out in the middle of nowhere, they serve up a really hardy breakfast. Do you think the two of you can muddle through until someone gets there?"

"Do you mean cook? Then yes. We can just make sure no one is seated in the middle of the place until you have people here. We're also going to need something to transport the people to our homes. I don't know what Dawson is planning." His brother told him what he wanted to do. "All right. He wants to take both the woman and her dad to his place to care for them. I'll help out when I can. But that's the plan."

"I like that plan. Don't you just love it when the stars line up or some shit like that? Anyway, there will be a cleanup crew there in about twenty minutes. They'll say there was a buckled floorboard, and that will keep people from wandering where they'd be best not to. Also, the staff will arrive one at a time over the next thirty." He thanked her. "Hang on a second. I'm looking into something. My oh my."

Thatcher put his phone on speakerphone when Rogen asked him to.

"If this is about my mate or her dad, I don't want to know. Not yet, at any rate." She told him it might be important. "All right. But just the important parts. Nothing personal."

"Caitlynn Leary is a grad from law school. Gave it all up to come to the States to be with her dad when he needed her about six months ago. Apparently, Shawn Leary has been having some kind of nightmare episodes for some time now. He fought in a couple of skirmishes back in Ireland and came to the States to start fresh when his wife was killed in an automobile accident about three years ago." Dawson asked her if this was considered important. "It is. Shawn is said to have murdered his wife and their unborn child and fled here to not just get a fresh start but to avoid prison. I'll look into that too. Also, you should know, Dawson, that the restaurant is about a week from closing down. Not that there isn't enough money—there is, but only barely—but a corporation has decided that the land would be better suited to their needs than the needs of having a hardy meal. Shawn apparently gives meals to anyone that comes in that needs one. They pay it off by doing dishes or something along those lines. It's made him a very popular person in that little town. I think I'm going to like this man."

"Me too."

The bell at the front of the place dinged, and Dawson went to answer it. Thatcher got up to start cooking after dragging Shawn to the other side of the kitchen. Rogen asked him to talk to her through their link.

All right. Two things you should know about Shawn and Caitlynn. First of all, Caitlynn is a hell of an attorney. She is currently taking some classes here to update her on Ohio laws. She's an international attorney and could fit well within our little circle. Also, Shawn was a surgeon while in Ireland. After his wife was killed, he just couldn't do it anymore. I think he might need his ass kicked back into gear. Shawn also speaks four languages, including Gaelic. Caitlynn speaks six. He asked her why she'd not been able to tell him that on the phone. *I thought when I heard the door ding that you might be needing both your hands. I forgot that your mom made sure you guys could cook.*

Dawson said he had a two-top that wanted to look over the menu. He handed him one of them so he'd know what to cook with each meal. Making sure he had all the things he might need for breakfast, he was surprised and charmed that there was a large pot of Irish oatmeal on a low burner.

She wanted to make sure we could survive on more than just fast food. There is something very nice about this menu, Rogen. Like Shawn decided he would cook the things he loved and fuck the rest of the norm. Irish oatmeal. There is quick toast here too. Mom used to make that when she had stale bread. Butter it up and put it in a skillet to warm it up. She said she thought she made that for the grandkids. *More than likely. Did you know that Mom is making sure that the grandkids can cook things? I love it.*

When Dawson brought back his order, he told him that the crew was there to clean up. Telling Rogen, he also told her that he had to go. Cooking required concentration. Enjoying himself for the first time since being called out yesterday, Thatcher decided he might just figure out a way to get this sort of cooking in town. He thought that if no one else would enjoy it, he certainly would. Thatcher thought his dad might as well. Whistling as he worked the grill, he was shocked to his very core when Caitlynn spoke behind him.

"What the bloody hell is going on here?"

Caitlynn didn't know what to think about the two men working with her, but she decided they were much too busy to worry over it now. Thatcher was doing a good job of keeping up with things, and Dawson was making sure the cash register was covered, as well as the breakfast bar that the regulars came in to be seated at. He was also having a wonderful time.

Her da was still lying on the floor in the kitchen. She was sure there was something going on with that, but for now, she didn't want to know. The amount of blood in front of the sinks was scary to her, and she decided she didn't want to look into it too deeply right now.

"Do you know what bubble and squeak is?" She stared at Thatcher when he asked her. "I could look it up, but I have a feeling your dad didn't go by any kind of recipe when it came to cooking back here. There are all kinds of things in his walk-in that make me think that he got what was on sale and made up his menu from that."

"You Americans call it fried potatoes. Cut the ones leftover in the icebox into small bits and fry them up." He thanked her. "There is fresh marmalade in the icebox too. What the hell is going on here? You're not a cook, are you?"

"I am right now. And there is a great deal going on that will take some time to tell you about. I will. And so will Dawson. But for now, I think we need to get this place fixed up, so the people aren't too suspicious about things." She didn't move, wondering if she should press the matter more. "I promise you, Caitlynn, we're going to tell you everything. I'm sure you have a great many questions. We'll get to those as well."

The blood on her shirt was something she kept coming back to. A large apron that her da usually wore was covering it up. Dawson had put ketchup on it too to make it look more like that sort of stain than blood. Caitlynn remembered being shot and wondered why she wasn't in more pain. Or dead, for that matter.

The breakfast crowd was served up faster than ever with the extra hands. Thatcher was doing a great job of putting out the food. Dawson was amazing at waiting tables, making coffee, and making sure that everyone had what they needed. While there was a couple of seconds between customers, he was making sure all the salt and pepper shakers were filled, as well as the little bowls of sugar packets. It was like having three extra people with him around, rather than just him.

Other people began to show up as they dealt with the crowd. Two of them went to the kitchen to help Thatcher with not just cleaning the pots and pans but to clear up the blood on the floor. Three more of them began taking tables to wait on and worked like they'd been doing it here for years. Caitlynn had a chance to sit down with a hot cup of tea when she was shoved into a seat. Dawson sat across from her.

"I don't know if I like you overly much. You're not only a better waitstaff than me, but you seem to be enjoying yourself too much." He grinned, and she felt her heart do a little flip flop. "You here to tell me what is happening?"

"I will answer anything you wish to know. Your accent is not as pronounced as it was when we first arrived." She told him the reason for that was that when she was upset, it came out stronger. And people expected her to have an accent when she was waiting on them. "Oh, well, that's sad. I like it. It suits you to have a fiery temper along with all that red hair. And the freckles are about the cutest thing I've seen."

"Behave, you idiot, before I smack you." He laughed, and she grinned in response. "I was shot. What happened that I'm not hurting at all. And so you know, I've looked—there isn't a wound or anything to be found either."

"Do you want this right upfront or working up to it? I can do either way." She said she liked her information like she liked her whiskey, straight up. "Good. When you were shot, it didn't look like you were going to make it. So I changed you into a cat. A tiger, to be exact. Thatcher changed your father into one too when he went into the kitchen and slit his wrists. It was touch and go there for a while for—"

"Back up. What do you mean, you've changed me into a cat? I'm not a cat." He only stared at her as he sipped his own tea. "Let me think on that a moment. So, you saved my life by changing me into a tiger. And my da too. Okay, I guess I don't mind that so much. So you're a shifter. I don't know many of them, to be honest."

"You were in contact with a bear, as well as a fox at some point recently. I can smell them on you." Nodding, she let what he was saying to her roll around in her mind. "I don't mean to spring this on you now, but you're also my mate. Do you understand what that means?"

"Yes. Somewhat. I'm an attorney or was one in Ireland. I did a couple of cases with a mate who had supposedly killed his mate or children. I got a book on shifters from the pack leader that helped me win the case. Also, a bear case. Bruin, I think they're called."

"Yes. We know a few bears. The pack leader in

our town is a good friend of the family as well." She thought about what he was telling her when Thatcher sat down with them. He had brought them a large platter of food and three forks. "This looks amazing, Thatcher. Did you make this?"

"Yes. It's an Irish breakfast. I'm not sure about the black pudding, but I put it in here to try. I had to look it up. It's not legal to sell or even to have in the States." Caitlynn explained why her da served it. "Okay, I didn't know that. Good idea to take regular sausage, and dying it black is a good way to get around that. And it's doubtful that anyone here would know the difference. Your dad is a smart man."

"He is. Will he be all right?" Dawson told her he would be better than he had been before. So would she be. "Why are all these people coming into work? I'm sure you had something to do with that too."

"Yes. I can't tell you any more than that until we get to know you better. But I will tell you that nothing we're doing is illegal, nor will it come back to bite you in the ass." Thatcher looked at her with a sort of cocky grin. "I can tell you that my wife, as well as the wives of my other brothers, works for some very important people. And that they'll make sure things are done in such a way that nothing will be able to hurt you or your father again."

"They accused him of killing my ma and unborn

sister. Da would never do anything like that." Neither of them so much as blinked. "Do you believe me or not? Now would be the time to tell me that so I can take care of him."

"I don't know anything about that. Nothing other than what my wife told us." Caitlynn nodded and looked around her da's restaurant to give herself time. "Rogen, my wife, told us that this place is going to be torn down in a couple of weeks. I'm sorry about that. You seem to be doing really well here."

"We were. I came home to help my da move to someplace else. He loves being in the kitchen. He told me it makes him not have to think about things much. I think he just likes tasting the food as he cooks it." She looked back at Dawson. "My da, he's all I have in the world, and I'd move the earth to make sure he's safe and cared for. He didn't mean to shoot me. He gets these night terrors that make it so he sleepwalks."

"Thatcher told me he's taking a lot of drugs, both prescribed and over the counter. I think he might be making himself ill by taking a couple of combinations of drugs that he shouldn't be taking. Did you know that?" She said she hadn't. "Also, I can set him up with someone to talk to about his nightmares. There are things that might be contributing to him having them that he's not being treated for."

"He doesn't see a psychiatrist. I tried to get him

into one, but he's not a citizen yet, so they won't set him up. It's been hard on him, too, with getting his medications. No insurance or any kind of help from anyone for the same reasons." Dawson said he'd take care of that for her. "You're just willing to jump right in with both feet and help out without knowing a thing about us? Why is that? Not to mention, I know nothing about you."

"You're my mate, as I told you. And I'd do anything, including taking a bullet for you should that be necessary. I wish I'd been in a position to do that for you earlier, but I think this works so much better for us." She asked him what his version of *us* meant. "Whatever you wish it to be. I have no intentions of rushing you into anything. And I'd never tell you to do something you wouldn't want to do on your own. I'm very laid back and easygoing. I'm a doctor that works with my brother. I have a few charities I work on as well. I have money, or I should say we have money. Everything I have is now yours. And whatever you have is also yours. I have five brothers, one of them being Thatcher. Five sisters-in-law that are married to them. Parents that I love deeply and profoundly. Nieces and nephews as well."

"What is it you're not telling me?" Dawson asked her what she meant when Thatcher got up to guide the men that were cleaning up into the back room for something to eat. "I don't know, Dawson. What sort of skeletons do you have hidden in your closet? Is there another wife? Never mind, that doesn't work with shifters. I feel like that rabbit going down the hole, and I've no idea what I'm going to fall into next."

"I don't know that I have any skeletons in my closet. But I can and will have Rogen look for you. As for the rabbit hole? I'm feeling the same thing. I've never had a mate before. Hadn't even thought of having one with the way things are going right now. I am happy about it. Excited to see what the rest of our lives turn out to be." She asked him about children. "I don't have any, as you might well know. However, if and when we have any, that would be entirely up to you, as it is your body."

"You're too nice. No one is this nice." He told her he thought she was looking for trouble. "More than likely, you're right on that. I'm working last night, and two men show up at the door. My da shoots me. You and your brother turn us into tigers, and now I find out I'm a cat. I think under the circumstances, I'm allowed to be looking for the other shoe to drop."

"I suppose you're right." A young man dressed in jeans and a tee came to sit with them for only a few seconds before he left a note behind and left them. She asked Dawson what it said when he put it back on the table. "Your father is loaded up and on his way to my home to recover. You'll stay there too, should you wish. I'm not there often, as I'm working a great deal nowadays. But I won't share a room or a bed with you until you say so. That doesn't mean I don't want to—I do, very much so—but I won't. The note also says that anytime you're ready to go, we can leave the restaurant in good hands."

She stood up and felt something run over her. Dawson put his hand out to steady her, but he didn't touch her. She had a feeling it was the cat in her but didn't comment. There was just too much other shit going on for her to worry about being a tiger right now.

Getting into the back seat of the car, she was surprised when Thatcher sat in the passenger seat, and Dawson drove. Looking out the window at the restaurant as it grew smaller and smaller, the lights dimmer too, Caitlynn wondered what the next phase of her life would be. And decided that she wasn't going to let some overgrown housecat ruin her life. She had it just the way she liked it.

The trouble was, she liked Dawson too. Very much. She didn't think she'd ever met a man like him and likely wouldn't again. Lying back on the seat, she let herself fall asleep. It was her superpower, her dad had told her. To be able to fall asleep no matter where she was or how she was positioned. Sleep was the best way to deal with things, she thought.

Chapter 9

Brooke didn't care for this. Not that she knew how to do it differently, but she didn't like people taking chances, huge ones, in this case, that might get them killed. Or if it turned out to be nothing. It couldn't be nothing, her mind told her. There were body parts all over the place. Brooke looked at Rogen when she said her name.

"It'll be fine. You'll see. Tru is there on-site, and there are about two dozen people that work for me that are going to be there in the event that shit hits the fan. It won't, but they're there in case it does." She supposed that being in the computer room with Rogen was about the safest place she could have been. But she still worried. "The building is right there where you said it would be. All kinds of people are interested in seeing what the fuck is going on. Once we breach the door, it'll be a piece of cake to see what is going on and putting an end to it."

"To it or the people in there?" Rogen told her it would be both if it turned out they were working on their own. "Otherwise, you'll keep them until they give up whatever information they have, then kill them?"

"No. They'll end up in prison. Killing them for helping won't get us anywhere. I like to give people a second chance." Brooke just cocked a brow at her. "Okay, I'm not into second chances, but I'm working to improve myself. A kid will do that to you, I guess."

A voice echoed around the room when the speaker clicked. "I'm to tell you that we have a hit on the owner of the land and building. He's been dead for nearly thirteen years." Rogen asked who was in charge, then. "His son, the best we can tell. He's been using the land as well as the property for some time now. There is a field of pot growing not ten minutes walking distance from where your men are."

"That was Winnie Donaldson. She's a good friend of mine, and also the person I report to. You will, too, when you get your head out of your ass and help us." Brooke told her she thought she was helping. "Nah, this is old shit you had. I mean full-time. The perks are great, and you get to see the world. With your ability to blend into any situation with your camera, it makes it nice for us. And the fact that you have a press license makes it all the better getting in and out of shit."

Rolling her eyes at the other woman, she looked at the screen when she did. Rogen was hard to get to know. All the women were hard-assed and hard to know. But she was beginning to see a side of them that she was sure few saw. They were mush when it came to the children in this place.

Thatcher came down with some glasses of tea, as well as two gallons of the stuff he put in the fridge.

As Rogen guided the men into position, she listened to Thatcher talking to her in low tones about what she was doing. When she saw something on the screen, she stood up and said for them to wait. The order was put out there that no one was to move as a family of four walked by some of the people hidden on the ground. They moved within two inches of one of the men she could see the outline of on the monitor.

"Christ, that was close." She agreed with the man on the monitor when he began to move toward the building when the all-clear was given. "We're leaving two behind to make sure there aren't any more visitors. Thanks for catching that."

Rogen winked at her, and she kept her eyes on the things that were surrounding the red outlines of people on the ground. Then the door was opened — such a mild word for the door exploding inward — and the windows broken in by the men entering the place.

There was a great deal of noise, along with the flash of lights that could be seen from the windows.

"Three Caucasian men inside working on what appears to be human remains." She nodded when Rogen looked at her. "There is a bandsaw in here that was being used when we entered, as well as a shit ton of large trash bags." The man in charge on the ground said nothing for several minutes. "They're stashing the clothing of the victims in them, it looks like. I have identification on the men here."

As he took pictures of the IDs of the men, he sent them from his phone to Rogen. As she looked them over, so did Brooke. "Do the faces of the people match the men in there?" Rogen asked them what she had. "Okay, the man named Fletcher Parker, can you let me see his face? Or something along those lines?"

His face suddenly appeared in front of her. The face, as clear as day, took up four of the monitors in front of her. She stared at the face for several seconds, then asked for the faces of the other two men. Rogen asked her what she saw.

"I don't know yet. I need to think on it." The other two men's faces seemed to ring a bell with her, and the work being done in the building resumed. It wasn't until Rogen was clearing the men to burn the building that she remembered something. "Wait. The first man, Parker. I remember him now. I've seen him in the town a couple of times when I was there working on getting into the country. He was known for having a hidey-hole in his business. It would contain things like money, credit cards, as well as passports. The other man, Liston, the second person you showed me, that's not his name either. He went by Morgenstern or something like that. He owned a butcher shop in town. Christ, now that I think on that and finding this, I'm so glad I didn't get anything from there. I don't remember the third man, but I have a feeling he has something to do with them in the food industry. Perhaps a restaurant or something."

"Found them. Six passports with different names on them, as well as money." The man showed them what he'd found and where it had been found. "You might also be interested in knowing there is paperwork that is used to put on meat when it leaves the country. Kinda sickening if you ask me, but I'm not a meat-eater."

The men worked the room over again, finding not only things that had been stashed but a great deal more money than they'd thought. It was Tru, going into the building after them, that found the letters. There were six in total.

"They're addressed from the two of you. I can open them if you wish, but I'd rather bring them back to you." Rogen agreed. "I'm bringing the cash with me, as well as the other stuff that was found. The men, I believe, were working for themselves. It looks as if, from the identifications that we found, they were killing tourists that were in town on vacation. Hell of a way to end your free time. Also, and I find this particularly funny, they have a diagram on the wall where the bandsaw is, telling how to cut the bodies up to look like what might be considered steaks or loins. Just around the back of this place is a large cast-iron cauldron that seems to be used for rendering fat. I don't even want to think about what that might have been used for."

"Are they saying anything?" Tru said she hadn't heard them but did ask the man behind her. He told her that since they'd broken the door down, all the men had done was get on their knees with their hands laced up on their heads. "Why are they smiling? I mean, would you be smiling if someone broke down your door and pointed guns to your face? They look so happy."

"You're right. Let me do something here and see what I can snap out of them." Whatever she did, there was no camera on them. When Tru came back online, she was showing her face, and Brooke could just make out the men on the floor behind her. One of them looked to be dead. His neck was broken. "Their father runs the town. They think they'll be out before we can process them. I'm thinking they don't understand what the hell they're up against with us. I'm having them taken to the plane now to bring back to a base that can deal with them. Good call, Brooke. You more than likely saved us a great deal of paperwork on this one. Thanks."

Rogen thanked her too. Thatcher handed her a candy bar, and she peeled it open while she thought about what she'd just done. She'd been helping her sisters-in-law out was how she was going to think about what had just happened. There was no way she'd been instrumental in any of the shit that had gone down. Brooke just happened to be in the right place at the right time.

She looked up when Jonas said her name.

"I must have zoned out for a minute. Where did everyone go?" He told her they were celebrating upstairs by ordering Chinese food. "I could eat that. Are we invited?"

"Yes." Jonas laughed. "I brought the kids with me when they called to tell me that you work for them now."

"I don't. I was helpful to them, but I don't work with them. I'd like to think that way for the time being." He nodded. "What else did I miss? I'm assuming there was more if they're celebrating."

"Yes. The government in the town where they were working has been arrested. Not just the father of the three you helped get, but several others that had a hand in what was going on. The restaurant, as well as the butcher shop, has been closed down. Rogen made sure the reason for the shutdown is printed in the local paper, as well as a sign put on each of the doors stating that they were using human remains as their products. I think that will be very telling in a couple of days. The third man, he was only there to help them get the stuff processed. Just as guilty, but he wasn't related to the other two."

"I saw him in the places the other two were in. I didn't connect him to them as he was wearing different hats, literally, at the time. What will happen to them?" He didn't say anything. "I guess I don't want to know. What do you know about Caitlynn?"

"She's taking care of her dad right now at Dawson's house. I've not met her, but Thatcher said she's a good person." Brooke nodded. "What's wrong? Something is there, and I'd gladly help you with it. Tell me so I can be your knight in shining armor."

"Your dad says that all the time to your mother. I don't know what's going on with me today. I should be thrilled, but I feel like I'm sort of the oddball out. The others work with Rogen. She's begged me to work too, but I don't know. She's very intense, and I thought I'd just as soon not get into a fight with her over anything. I don't think Rogen plays fair, do you?" He told her he wasn't going to answer that. "Yes, I can understand that too. She's very good at breaking into homes without leaving this office. Anyway, I was hoping Caitlynn and I could sort of make our own group of helpers. Not on the scale that the others are on, but more local things."

"I can get behind that. What is it you had in mind?" Brooke told him she didn't know right now. "There are a number of charities I have going on right now. So does Dawson. Maybe you and Caitlynn can work with us on a few of them."

"I'd like that anyway. I was thinking of trying to bring more businesses to the area. There are a great deal of unemployed families around that could use a boost. I know your family has the food drives, as well as helping the schools with supplies. But I think having a job would go a long way in making sure their kids know there is more to life than just handouts. Does that make sense?" He told her it did. Very much so. "Anyway. I have a lot of contacts I worked with. Mostly they're businesses that are expanding to other areas that aren't here. I can talk to them. I'd have to learn what is here for them to use, but I don't think that would be an issue."

"I can get you a list of properties we own, as well as a few tracks of land that are up for sale that we can purchase as a group and let companies know about. I know a great deal of things behind the scenes, so to speak, that the others might not know about. Being the accountant/investment person for the family affords me a great deal of information that I keep notes on." She smiled at him, thinking of all the things they could do with just that knowledge. "You look beautiful when you smile like that. You're beautiful anyway, but when you smile, you light up a room and my heart."

"You're very romantic. I hope you know that. And that you teach our sons that as well. Women swoon over that crap." He laughed and picked her up out of the chair. "I guess we need to get up there before they eat all the dumplings. I love those suckers."

The food was being delivered just as they entered the dining room. She was amazed at the amount of food and asked if there would be a lot of leftovers. No one moved — a pin could have been heard falling to the floor. Then they all burst out laughing as if she'd made a grand joke.

"We don't have leftovers in this house." Dawson kissed her on the cheek as he walked by her. Caitlynn was in the room already, handing out plates as people walked by her. Picking up the napkins, she placed one on each of the plates as they went by her. Dawson laughed, and she noticed that Caitlynn watched his every move.

"Does it get any easier? Being around so many large men?" Brooke told her she didn't even notice them anymore. "I would suppose it would be something to get used to. I'm Caitlynn. You must be Brooke, Jonas's mate."

"I am. I'm glad to meet you." They worked together like they were for another three minutes before they both realized they were missing the food. "How's your dad doing? Jonas told me you hopped right up after being changed. That's amazing."

"Dawson said it was because I was mortally wounded. I don't know how I feel about being a cat yet. You're not." She said she wasn't yet. "It's sort of strange, having this other half of me that's right there. I can feel her when I'm close to Dawson. Like she wants me to rub all over him. I'm not going to. Not yet, at any rate, but she's right there."

"Rogen told me once that it's strange having something there too. She was changed like you were in an effort to save her life." They had piled up their plates and were sitting down by then. Dawson was talking to Jonas when he turned and winked at her. "What is it you do for a living? I mean, before coming here?"

"Attorney. Then when my da came here and opened a restaurant, I missed him a great deal. After a while, he asked me to come to help him out with it, and I jumped at the opportunity. I think he'll miss that a great deal. Cooking for others." Brooke told her they could find him a place here to open a restaurant. "Really? He'd love that. I'm not sure how much he enjoyed cooking so much as talking to people. He's a talker when he has someone to listen."

"Then he'll love Thatch, their father. He'll talk a person's arm off." They were laughing when she told her what she had in mind for them to work together. "I don't know much just yet, but I know that helping out families isn't enough. We need some businesses to come in and hire a few hundred people."

They talked for hours about different things. Jonas brought her a pad of paper and a pen so she could keep up. Dawson joined them a few minutes after that and told them what he had in mind for the town.

~*~

Jonas played with Marie, Morgan's little girl until she yawned for the third time. He was joining her in her exhaustion too. He and Brooke had been up late the night before making love and then again earlier this morning. Yawning when she did, this time, the little girl let her eyes drift closed and stayed there. He looked up when his dad sat down across from him on the floor.

"I got something I want to talk to you about." Jonas felt his spine stiffen for whatever he'd done wrong for his dad to be upset with him. "I have me an idea about some things them girls have their heads together about. Improving things around here."

"Did you talk to them about it?" He said he wanted to run it by him first. "They're working on the town, Dad. I honestly don't know what they're planning."

"I know that. But this idea I have, it's a little off the path of getting any kind of improvements. I want to start me up one of them after-school things. Where kids can come in and mentor some of the younger kids on how to do stuff." He asked him what sort of stuff. "You know. Basketball. Maybe help with some homework. I don't know, son. I was just thinking on it. Might be able to get a ball game or two out of them if they want to. Also, a pool. Not one of ours, but one the city can put in. For swimming lessons and the like."

"I love the idea. However, you should be aware that putting in a pool is costly. Not the putting it in part, but insurance and hiring people to be there to watch over things. I mean, it's a good way to get some of the kids working in the summer, but I doubt it's in the budget for them to pay for the insurance. We could help out the first few years, but that sort of defeats the purpose of it being a city thing." Dad said he'd not thought of that. "I think it's something we can look into. I really like the idea of a community pool. And the fact that it will have to hire some kids around the town too. I just had a thought. Shawn, Caitlynn's father, loves to cook. Maybe he can make a concession stand work for the pool too."

"Now there we go. I like that idea." Dad told him of the places where he thought a pool might work. "I don't think putting it near the schools would be such a good idea. I don't know if I could live with myself if one of them kiddies got themselves hurt going there when they're not supposed to. But there are a couple of places that might work out."

He and his dad talked for an hour on the different spots he'd thought of. Jonas pulled out his cell after putting Marie on her blanket to sleep. Telling Dad of the couple of places that he knew were for sale that might work, they decided to get with someone to see about purchasing it. That was about the time that Caitlynn and Brooke joined them.

"What a lovely house this is. I'm betting it cost a pretty penny too." Dad laughed. "What do you have to think is so funny, dear sir? It's a good deal more than I have. You can bet your ass about that."

"I'm sure it is. But since I don't care so long as we can all get together like this, it could be worth billions, and I'd not care. I'm these here boys daddy. You're Dawson's mate." She said that remained to be seen yet. "Well, if you're knowledgeable to any of our kind, you know that's a done deal."

"Dad. You're not making any friends here."

He asked him what he meant, and Jonas nodded at Caitlynn. "You're pissing her off. Back off on telling her it's a done deal or she'll hit you."

"They already met, so it's done as far as I'm concerned. I'm just telling her the truth of it." Dad looked at Caitlynn and smiled. "You're not mad at this old man, are you?"

"I am, as a matter of fact. Nothing is a done deal, as you put it unless I say it is. Your son is a good deal smarter than you are if you think just because he's my mate, I'm going to lie down with my legs spread out and tell him to come and get it." Dad's face turned a nice shade of purple. He was so embarrassed. Caitlynn stood up. "Don't ye be saying things like that to me again, old man or I'll make you regret you opened your eyes this morn. Done deal. I'll tell you what's a done deal—it's me dealing with men like you. I'm a grown fucking woman, and I decide when I want someone to come to my bed. You just remember I'm not a broodmare that needs a man to order me around."

When she left, Dad looked at him. "I didn't mean it like that. I was just meaning that she was his mate, and they'd have to be together, or he'd go insane." Jonas told him he should have started with that. "Do you think she's a might touchy? I didn't mean it."

"Dad, you're going to have to learn that the women of this family aren't like the women you grew up with. They marry who they want when they want. Or not at all. No one needs another person telling them what they should be doing at any time. Otherwise, the entire female population is going to come gunning for you."

They both heard Rogen say, "He said *what* to you?" and Jonas shook his head.

"Take my advice, Dad. Just keep saying you're sorry, or you're never going to get out of the doghouse."

Getting up, taking Marie with him, he left his dad to deal with the women. They were all headed to the living room when he walked out. He didn't envy his dad right now. Either he'd be in trouble for the rest of his very short life if they had anything to say about it, or he'd be buying out the florist in pretty flowers to make up for it for the rest of his days.

"Your dad is in trouble." Jonas kissed Brooke on the mouth and told her he knew. "I thought about rescuing him, but he's said the same thing to me. He really is in the dark ages if he thinks that what he can say and not say won't ruffle some feathers. It didn't bother me because I've gotten used to him, but Caitlynn is new." She reached for the baby Jonas was holding. "Let me hold her."

Marie was awake now and clung to Brooke like she'd wanted a break from him too. The two of them sat there talking about nothing at all, but Marie seemed to be hanging onto her aunt's every word. When she sat her on the table to give her some of the little pieces of rice left on her plate, Brooke spoke to him.

"I decided that I'd like to have a child with you. Soon. Not right away, but whenever we can get around to it." He laughed and told her how it worked. "Okay, when I go into heat. There is another archaic-sounding statement. Heat. I suppose you call it breeding too."

"We do, as a matter of fact. Not to any of the women, but that's what we say when we're trying to keep our nuts where they are. What changed your mind?" She told him. "Yes, I can see where being around babies a great deal can make you want one of your own. But you must remember that we can't just leave them with their parents when we leave this place. We will be taking them with us."

She laughed at him. "Your mom, she was telling me about some of the ornaments you boys made her when you were children. And you are the only one that has kept that tradition up of giving her one every Christmas." Jonas told her how he had already picked one out for her for this year but now wanted to change it. "Because of us, you mean?"

"Yes. I find an ornament that goes with an event that happened in the year. Last year I got her a beautiful cruise ship. She and Dad had gone on a cruise that they loved. The year before that, I got her an apple tree with bright yellow apples on it. Mom discovered fuji apples at the market and went on about them for weeks after." She asked him what he'd get for the two of them from her. "I don't know. I have to find something to do with the two of us. Something that shows we're a couple."

"Why not get her one that shows all her sons mated to women? Perhaps one that names the children. No, that wouldn't work. That would have to be redone all the time. But the couples, that would be nice. I would love it." He said he knew just the place to get it. "It would also be really great if we could gather everyone up and get their picture taken. I could do that. And then one of your parents. It would be simple enough to put them in with their family. Make it a large photo that would hang over their fireplace."

"I wonder if Houston would want to paint it." She said that would be epic for them. "I'm liking this more and more all the time. And no dressing up for it. We will take the picture as we are daily. My dad said he didn't like family portraits that showed off this well-dressed family when people don't look like that all the time."

"I like that too. Oh, this will be wonderful. We'll have to get on it soon. In order for Houston to get to paint it, I have to take the pictures and then put them together. For everyone else, we should take individual pictures of them as well with their kids this year. Make

it a family tradition to get together for their families."
Jonas kissed her again — this was going to be wonderful.
"You contact your brothers and find out what time
would be best. My hands are itching to get started on
this."

By the time they were ready to leave, he'd
gotten all of them to agree to come by his place to
get the pictures of all of them together tomorrow at
noon. Brooke thought the fall colors would be perfect
as a background, and he was as excited as she was.
Houston came to them right away after they asked him
if he wanted to paint it and hugged Brooke tightly.

Dad came into the dining room looking like a
beaten man. Brooke asked if he was all right, and Dad
told her he wasn't sure. Patting him on the hand then
kissing his cheek, he told her that certainly helped.

"Jonas and I were just talking about children."
That perked his dad right up. "The next time I go into
heat, something I'd not mention to Caitlynn if I were
you, we're going to try for a baby."

"I'm not going to say a word from now on. I
never in my life thought I'd be insulting someone by
just talking. I'll show them. They'll have to beg me to
speak to them from now on." Dad took Marie off the
table and cuddled her. "You'll love your old granddad,
won't you, honey? Me and your sister will be having a
blast soon as the weather gets warmer again."

When dad walked away, still talking to the little girl in his arms, Jonas looked at Brooke when she laughed. "He might just do it too. I hope he does. I think, myself, that he didn't mean any harm, but that's just me. She'll blend in or not. If not, we'll never find her body. Are you ready to go home?"

He was laughing as they made their way to the car. Brooke was a pistol and would keep him on his toes for some time. Driving to his home, he wondered what it would be like to have a bunch of his own kids running around. Well, he thought, soon enough. Soon enough, he'd know.

Before You Go...

HELP AN AUTHOR

write a review

THANK YOU!

Share your voice and help guide other readers to these wonderful books. Even if it's only a line or two, your reviews help readers discover the author's books so they can continue creating stories that you'll love. Log in to your favorite retailer and leave a review. Thank you.

Kathi Barton, a winner of the Pinnacle Book Achievement Award and a best-selling author on Amazon and All Romance books, lives in Nashport, Ohio, with her husband, Paul. When not creating new worlds and romance, Kathi and her husband enjoy camping and going to auctions. She can also be seen at county fairs with her husband, who is an artist and potter.

Her muse, a cross between Jimmy Stewart and Hugh Jackman, brings her stories to life for her readers in a way that has them coming back time and again for more. Her favorite genre is paranormal romance, with a great deal of spice. You can visit Kathi online and drop her an email if you'd like. She loves hearing from her fans. aaronskiss@gmail.com.

Follow Kathi on her blog: http://kathisbartonauthor. blogspot.com/